The Dark Side

DARKENING

For Amy – with
grateful thanks
and much love

Ashe

ASHE BARKER

Darkening
ISBN # 978-1-78184-643-8
©Copyright Ashe Barker 2013
Cover Art by Posh Gosh ©Copyright July 2013
Interior text design by Claire Siemaszkiewicz
Total-E-Bound Publishing

Published in 2013 by Total-E-Bound Publishing, Think Tank, Ruston Way, Lincoln, LN6 7FL, United Kingdom.

DARKENING

Dedication

This book is dedicated to John and Hannah, for putting up with me.

Prologue

"Red. Red. Enough. Stop now, please!"

Shit! Not again…

Nathan doesn't voice his frustration out loud — with some considerable effort — but he knows the rules and honours the safe word immediately. Taking a deep breath, and with a last rueful glance at the naked, quivering and only very slightly pink buttocks of his latest she-said-she-was-oh-so-willing partner, he places the barely used spanking paddle on a side table behind him. Reaching around with his left hand, he loosens the straps restraining the cringing blonde, who has now started to sob prettily. Using his right arm, he supports her around the waist to stop her imminent descent to the floor as he frees first her wrists, then her ankles.

Taking her weight, Nathan lifts the girl from the dark brown leather sofa, across the back of which he'd strapped her so carefully only minutes earlier. He carries her across the room to deposit her face down on his large bed, remarkably gently given his darkening mood. He dumps a box of tissues beside her.

"Dry your eyes, Susanna. We're finished." *Sniff, sniff, whimper, whimper. Christ!*

He has deliberately softened his voice. No point taking his frustration out on Susanna. She's tried her best — probably. Possibly.

"You can get dressed. Unless you want to take a shower first. Then I'll phone you a taxi."

He congratulates himself on managing to keep a lid on his mounting frustration, inwardly cringing at the tears and sniffling. He's not entirely convinced by the display of grief and shock — the lovely Susanna is not above a spot of scheming and manipulation to get her own way, he's sure of that — but still, he isn't in the business of making women cry. Not really. Cry *out*... Now, that's different.

He might be a dab hand with a cane, he definitely likes to hear them scream, but all this sobbing? No. He wants his subs to look back rather more fondly on his attentions than he suspects Susanna will. He prefers them to be more appreciative of the pain he can inflict, and the pleasure, and to leave his apartment humming.

But hey, what do you know? The lovely Susanna is already beginning to rally. In fact her sudden, rapid and pretty much total recovery before his very eyes seems little short of miraculous, given the quivering mess that was draped across his sofa just moments ago. She is starting to sniff daintily and is now obligingly rolling over onto her back, her arms flung up onto the pillow to show off her curvy little pink-tipped breasts to best advantage.

Sitting alongside her on the edge of the bed, and still fully dressed apart from his black, soft leather jacket and navy tie, Nathan signals with a flick of his finger that she should stay face down. The view is definitely not without its attractions, but, in truth, his interest in her breasts—or indeed any other part of her anatomy—is at an irrevocable end.

He reaches into a drawer beside the bed for the large tub of Savlon he keeps there. Unscrewing the lid, he takes a generous scoop of the soothing cream onto his fingers and starts to spread it across her backside. As gently as he is able in his current frustrated state, he works the cream into her buttocks. They were just beginning to glow nicely, in his view, and could use a couple of dozen more strokes to bring her sweet little arse to full tenderness, ready for a good, hard, satisfying fuck.

Time to call a halt, he acknowledges ruefully. *Susanna just isn't going to cut it as a submissive. Pity, but there you are...*

Snatching a couple of tissues from the box on the bed, he wipes his hands. He stands, gazing down from his height of six-two at the undoubtedly lovely blonde stretched out on his bed...and realises he just wants her out of here. Now.

Tunnelling his fingers through his over-long dark hair—he usually pulls it back into a sleek ponytail, but he prefers to let it hang loose to his shoulders when he's in Dom mode—he ponders the mysteries of women. And, in particular, what brought Susanna, decked out in a very fetching black and red leather corset and thong, along to The Manor House, that exclusive club in leafy, suburban north Leeds. There, she paraded around in front of him until he eventually beckoned her over and treated her to the spanking she was obviously looking for.

That went well enough—she seemed to appreciate his efforts and he certainly saw promise there. She obligingly agreed to meet him the following week. They had coffee together at Starbucks in City Square, discussed his requirements—his *exact* requirements—and she agreed to join in his 'games'.

He's always very explicit regarding what he has in mind. Over the years he has found it best to avoid any misunderstanding up front. Susanna is no exception. His submissives need to agree, willingly, to do what he asks. Indeed, it's always something of a surprise to him that some even offer more. Again, Susanna is a case in point, having suggested that a nice bit of age regression could offer an interesting twist to their bondage and discipline play.

Not to Nathan, it wouldn't—not his idea of fun at all. He turned her down politely but very firmly. But if she's so keen on gymslips and canes, why has she wimped out at the first sight—well, seventh stroke, actually, in this evening's case—of a very unassuming spanking paddle?

He had a lot more than that planned for her over the coming few weeks. She is absolutely gorgeous, just his favourite type of submissive. Not that he has a particular physical preference. He doesn't care whether they are blonde, brunette, with blue eyes, green or brown, tall or petite, slender or curvy. Well, if he's honest he does have a fondness for willowy redheads, probably because they tend to be fair-skinned so their buttocks go a beautiful, delicate shade of pink without too much effort on his part. Although he's flexible regarding physical appearance, Nathan does go for a particular demeanour. Privately, he calls it his 'librarian look'. He likes submissives who present themselves as meek and modest, unassuming, studious, quiet, shy. They can be plain—but preferably not too plain—dress as if they are going to a funeral, wear bottle-bottom glasses—you can always remove glasses, he's found, if they get in the way of a blindfold—and not say boo to a goose. The fun comes from peeling back those layers to reveal the sexy, demanding, responsive little temptress underneath, the slut under the prim and proper outer shell. He loves to transform his subs from demure Sunday School teachers to panting sex goddesses in a matter of minutes. Female orgasms are absolutely the biggest turn on Nathan Darke can ever imagine—he loves it when they come.

He particularly loves how women sound when caught up in ecstasy—their soft, breathy moans, groans, panting. And screaming. He particularly likes to hear a woman scream, so he doesn't use gags that often. And he loves the writhing and stretching as a woman spreads herself out under him or in front of him, even when she's bound and blindfolded, completely open to his touch and revelling in all he offers. And that sublime moment when they reach the point where they're begging him to fuck them—hard and fast and often. He aims to please, and as far as he's aware no woman has ever left his bed disappointed.

Until now. Susanna is definitely not happy, and distinctly disappointed. To be fair, he's pretty disappointed in her too—he had such high hopes for her. By way of celebration once she agreed to join in his 'games', and by way of partial compensation for his intransigence over the gymslip, he invested in a new set of canes to add to his already extensive collection, as well as two neon-coloured butt plugs, all with her delicious little arse particularly in mind.

But she's safe worded—again. This is her third visit to his apartment and each time she's cut their games short. Well short.

He glances back at the bed. It's obvious that the cream has been absorbed into Susanna's peachy little butt-cheeks and done its work. The crying, wincing, wittering and sniffling have all stopped, and Susanna now seems perfectly calm and collected. She obviously enjoyed his ministrations, if her stretching and sighing was anything to go by. In fact, now she's really rather perky and keen to regroup. *Such amazing powers of recovery!* Nathan smiles wryly. Manipulative? Yes, probably.

Rolling onto her back to make sure he can properly appreciate her pale, slender body and full breasts, and opening her legs wide to make sure he's under no illusions about how wet and ready she is, Susanna smiles and runs her tongue slowly over her bottom lip.

"Thanks for stopping. I just got a bit, well, nervous really. I don't mind trying again in a minute as long as you don't hit me too hard..."

By way of invitation, Susanna rises to her knees on the bed, rubbing her own backside with one hand and using her other to roll first her right nipple, then her left until both are swollen and hard, pink, juicy pebbles. She arches her back to better present her breasts for him to suckle, if he cares to. She slides her hand downwards, between her legs. She's all happy smiles, bobbing breasts, throbbing clit and simpering apologies—and much to Nathan's astonishment, he wants none of it.

No doubt picking up on his lack of interest, she's now trying to placate him, offering to let him tickle her dainty, delectable little butt with his spanking paddle if he absolutely must, or better still suck her nipples, in exchange for a good fuck. It's clear enough to Nathan what she wants, and to be fair, she isn't being particularly unreasonable. Good, hot vanilla sex, maybe spiced up a bit, isn't such a bad offer.

But that's pretty much all that Susanna is offering. He's treated her to some fabulously explosive orgasms in their two previous encounters, and she obviously fancies a bit more of that, but on her terms.

Well, maybe if they'd met in a bar, or at the gym. But not on his turf. It's his terms that count here.

If Susanna wants vanilla she can have it — is welcome to it — but she's simply come to the wrong place looking for it. To the wrong man. He needs a submissive, and one with a hell of a lot more staying power than Susanna has demonstrated up to now, one who will hand over her body and let him do what he wants to it. A submissive who will explore his wants and fantasies with him, meeting his particular and sometimes brutal needs as well as her own.

And clearly Susanna is so not submissive. Submissives are exactly that, as far as he's concerned. They're partners who agree to submit, to voluntarily give themselves and their bodies over to him to do as he wants. They do this because it's safe, they know the deal, the parameters, and they trust him to take care of them.

And because they fucking love it, of course. Subs get off on it all, just as he does. The violence, the restraints, the beatings, the violation, the intimidation, the subjugation, the humiliation, submitting to his authority, the pretence of powerlessness...

She likes the sex well enough, and has all the modesty of a panther in heat once her black skirt and crisp white blouse hit the floor — she works as a solicitor's clerk in one of the commercial developments close to his apartment. *Classic librarian.* As well as being very handy — she can show up within a few minutes of his call — she will come on command, in any position, can play his cock like a musical instrument with her delicate little fingers and hot little mouth and she has the most receptive arse he can remember sinking his dick into in a long time. And she can keep going for hours. He definitely appreciates stamina.

The first time he brought Susanna here they went through exactly what he wanted from her, again. Susanna knew exactly what would be going on, her part in it, his very particular requirements. If a sub wants to stop at any time she can use a safe word of her choosing and that will do it. No argument, no questions. The deal is that he will stop immediately. If she is getting close to her limit and feels she can't take much more she can 'amber light' and he will respect that, maybe let up a little, take how she's feeling into account, help her to avoid having to safe word. There was absolutely no coercion. Never. He and Susanna talked it through, she didn't seem to have any questions — well, she didn't ask any when he offered her the chance — she didn't ask for any practices to be taken out or limited, expressed no reservations at all, and she couldn't get started fast enough.

Susanna is very enthusiastic and experienced, which has been a definite plus — regardless of his preference for the 'librarian look' he really can't do with naïve little virgins for what he has in mind. But it seems that despite all her 'qualifications' and feigned enthusiasm for spiced-up fucking, Susanna is really a vanilla at heart. She likes her sex straight and safe, minus the whistles and bells and with plenty of penetration.

Nothing wrong with that. It's just that he doesn't—well, apart from the penetration—so that's that.

Three strikes and you're out, sweetheart. No pun intended...

But you can't win 'em all.

Philosophical, he decides it'll be better to cut his losses with Susanna now. She's bloody lovely, truly she is, but not for him. He glances ruefully back at her, still stretched temptingly on his bed. Maybe he can just...for old times' sake?

But he squashes that notion fast. It would be a pity fuck at best. And, even more disturbing, he isn't entirely sure which of them would be on the receiving end.

"Do you want a shower, Susanna, or do you just want to get dressed?" he repeats, ingrained courtesy coming to the fore now, whatever the circumstances. "Are you hungry? A drink, maybe?" He's conscious that she came to the apartment straight from work, probably hasn't eaten. "I can fix you something if you like. Or I can just phone you a taxi?"

Not without some lingering regrets at a fine opportunity passed up, he turns his back on Susanna's little floorshow and strolls across the room towards an oak dressing table in an alcove, to retrieve his expensive gold watch and even more expensive platinum cufflinks.

"But it's not even nine o'clock yet. We've got hours." In the dressing table mirror he catches her delicate little shake of those tantalising breasts, just to emphasise the point and get his attention back. It works, up to a point. *Maybe vanilla has its attractions – I shouldn't be too dismissive after all...*

"I could stay over if you like..."

Her words bring him back to the reality of the situation. *Pity fuck? No, best not.* As he rolls down his shirtsleeves and re-threads the cufflinks, he tries to let her down as gently as he can, but he wants no further misunderstanding.

"No, Susanna, this isn't working. I'm tired — it's been a long day. I want to go home, and I think it's best if you do too." Turning back to face her, he tries a few soothing platitudes, tries to soften the blow. She's leaving, no doubt about that, but if he can he prefers to let her walk out of his apartment with her dignity intact. Not least, the last thing he wants is a disgruntled ex-sub badmouthing him at The Manor House and in his other networks. His reputation as a good, satisfying Dom means a lot to him, guarantees him plenty of ready and willing partners. Unhappy, complaining submissives do nothing to enhance it.

"You're gorgeous and sexy and we've had a good time. A fantastic time. But — you're obviously not cut out for what I have in mind." Gesturing towards his specially designed sofa, the inbuilt restraints still dangling where he left them, he goes on, "This isn't really your thing, is it?"

Susanna's response is just a malevolent glare and stony silence. How did he not notice that malicious gleam in her beautiful blue gaze before? There's no missing it now. Despite his best efforts at conciliation, this is a woman scorned. *Shit!*

Picking up her clothes from where they're scattered around the floor, he returns to the bed. She arrived wearing a plain white blouse, tailored black wool knee-length skirt and, underneath, a delightful pillar-box red lace bra with matching tiny panties. She knows how he likes her to look, on the surface and below, but not how he needs her to perform, it would seem. With a rueful last glance at the sofa, the dangling straps a reminder of his thwarted evening's entertainment, Nathan holds the clothes out to her, tries for some shred of reconciliation. "No hard feelings, love. Do you want me to leave you alone so you can get dressed in peace?"

"We had a deal…"

"And it's not worked out this time. Some deals just don't. We're not compatible—we want different things. So I honestly think it's best if we part company here. There are loads of guys out there who'd love to be with you. But I'm not looking for a girlfriend—if I was, you would be top of the list." *Well, in the top half, perhaps. Maybe.* "It's a submissive I'm looking for, and that's not what you want. Not really. Is it? So, still friends?"

More glaring, more angry silence. Nathan makes one last attempt. "And now, it's time to get dressed. Please."

Susanna's beautiful face hardens. Realising he means it, that he's actually about to throw her out of his apartment, she starts to protest in earnest.

"I've done what you wanted, let you tie me up and knock me about a bit. Like you said you wanted. And what do you mean, 'go home'? I thought this was your apartment. You live here."

"No, Susanna. It *is* my apartment, but I don't live here. Not usually."

"So what is this place, then? Your fuck pad?"

On a good day. "I suppose you could call it that. But there's not going to be any fucking here tonight. Time to go, Susanna."

Ignoring the blouse and skirt that Nathan has dropped onto the bed, she pulls on the underwear and stands before him, ready for a slanging match, all hands on hips and outraged frustration.

Oh God, now she's going to make a fuss.

"I don't mind it a bit rough, I told you that before. It adds to the excitement. But it's you. You're a kinky, sadistic bastard with your whips and canes, and this bloody room you've got kitted out like a torture chamber. You scare me, and you're gonna kill someone before you're done."

That's it, game over. Tried nice, not working.

Holding up one hand to interrupt the 'hell hath no fury' flow of invective, Nathan interrupts quietly. "If you've finished, I'll wait for you outside."

Turning on his heel, he picks up his leather jacket from the back of a chair and heads out of the door, then closes it softly behind him. The crash behind him might well be the Savlon tub hitting the door, but he'll check and clear up later, once she's gone.

Time to think about another visit to The Manor House. Maybe I should ask for references next time.

Chapter One

Don't you just love Beethoven?

Well, I do. I always have, since I was tiny. I'm just drifting along nicely to his Symphony Number 3 in E-flat major and contemplating the heroic doings of Napoleon Bonaparte—apparently Beethoven's inspiration for this particular symphony—as my mobile starts trilling. Definitely need to choose a new ringtone sometime soon—this din could be mistaken for a budgie caught in a car door. What could I have been thinking, choosing that? Napoleon never had ringtones to contend with. Neither did Ludwig van. And I don't appreciate the interruption.

It's not even seven o'clock in the evening yet, and I am curled up in bed. I am surrounded by archaeology textbooks although I'm not in the mood for serious reading, and I do have Ludwig for company. But still—in bed by seven and trying to teach myself about the mysteries of ancient Egypt out of sheer boredom is just pathetic. I so need to get a life.

The phone has somehow disappeared under the duvet. I know it's there somewhere because the budgie's still screaming its silly head off. It gets louder after a few rings. God, what overpaid nerdy whiz-kid thought that little gimmick up? A pushy phone—that's all I need. I get enough nagging from my mother. *'I just want what's best for you, dear…'*

"Sod ringtones." Now I know I'm losing it, because I'm actually talking to myself. I suppose the real danger sign is if I start answering. An uncomfortable thought. I shudder as I shove it brutally aside. *I'm fine, absolutely fine. Now.*

On that thought, I finally get my hands on the screeching HTC spawn of Lucifer and drag it out to face the light, punch the passcode into the keypad and answer.

"Hello, Eva Byrne…?" Always that expectant little pause, my name turned into a question as though I might not after all be me. Wishful thinking.

"Eva…? Evangelica, is it…? Ange, is that you? It's Natasha…" A little pause, no doubt to give me time to remember who Natasha might be. It doesn't work—my mind's a complete blank. And no one I know calls me Ange. Or Evangelica—unless it's my mother in a very bad mood.

"…from the agency."

Right, *that* Natasha. The snooty bitch with fuck-me heels and killer red talons glued onto her fingernails who looked at me like I was a lesser life form when I called in at the Little Maestros musical tuition agency a couple of weeks ago. I was looking for some alternative way of making a living, and if I could find something I actually liked doing, so much the better. I love music, and I quite like teaching, so I dropped off my CV and qualifications with a few agencies, just in case they might have some temp work going somewhere. Natasha looked a fraction more respectful when she spotted my first class honours degree in music from King's College, London, but rather spoilt the effect by asking me for proof of identity. Obviously she thought I'd stolen the degree certificate.

On reflection, I think her suspicions were aroused by my skinny black jeans, No Fear grey hoodie and psychedelic Converse trainers, topped off by a mop of wavy — or should that just be plain frizzy — red hair falling to the middle of my back. I'm not your archetypal music teacher.

My unruly hair is a constant nuisance, the bane of my life. It bounces, frizzes and waves everywhere, and short of shaving it off I have never found a way of controlling it. When I was a child my mother tried everything to get it into some semblance of order, and brushing it every morning became a war of attrition. The hair was winning, hands down, until eventually my mother had one of her Hiroshima moments where she takes decisive, drastic and usually disproportionate action. She marched me along to The Cutting Shop down on Stamford Hill High Street and had the lot chopped off. It curled more than ever in defiance after the vicious assault, but at least it would fit under a hat.

At five-four in heels and looking about sixteen — I am twenty-two, but like to tell myself I have worn well — I guess I didn't fit the image of a serious violin teacher as I perched in a trendy little black leather bucket chair in front of Natasha's pristine white desk, while she sneered down her aristocratic nose at me and suggested I was an impostor.

I wasn't especially desperate to impress Natasha the super-bitch — other agencies are available — so she was treated to my scruffy, sullen teenager look. Maybe my unpromising first impression was why it took her so long to get back to me. Oh, well—I need the work so I'd better make an effort now. If humble and well-mannered is called for, that's what I'll do.

"Ah—hello, Natasha, how are you?" Always polite, that's me, whatever the provocation. It's my mother's influence.

"There's a job come up you might be interested in." She pauses to let this sink in, make sure I'm listening. "Music tutor to an eight-year-old girl. She's learning the violin."

I am listening, and suddenly I'm very interested. I need to get a life, we've already established that, and here's one that might just do. I really want a job as a musician if possible, at least for now. I'm not bothered about earning much, and I know that private tuition is hardly going to keep me in shampoo and tampons, especially with the agency creaming off most of the fee. But with my somewhat unique talents I can earn enough in a single evening to cover pretty much anything I might need. This job sounds just right, just what I'm looking for. I can play a mean violin—shouldn't be too difficult to teach a little girl the basics. I put Ludwig on pause for a few minutes and resolve to be very polite indeed to Natasha.

Natasha rushes on with her explanations, obviously in a hurry and clearly desperate, which is probably why she's ringing me. "Valerie was doing it."

Valerie—do I know a Valerie?

"She's been teaching her for the last three months, but she busted her leg skiing and she's laid up somewhere in the French Alps."

French Alps—all right for some... But still, she's got a broken leg and now I've got her job, so I guess life sort of levels itself out.

Natasha is still gushing on. "Our contract with the client says we'll provide a replacement, and you're it. If you want to, of course... I need to know now, though, because we've already blobbed for two days and the client is not best pleased."

No need to ask me twice—I'm sold. "I'll do it. When do they want me, and where is it?"

"Ah, well, that's the thing. You start tomorrow, at nine—the client is very definite about that. Doesn't want little...whatever her name is...ah, yes, Rosie, little Rosie, missing any more of her lessons just because of a broken femur."

Sounds reasonable. "Okay, give me the address."

"Black Combe, Oakworth."

"Where?" Quick flick through my mental A–Z of London—nope, no Black Combe that I know of. Probably one of the new high-rises in the Docklands. Can't place Oakworth either, come to think. But not to worry, that's what satnavs are for.

"Oakworth. It's in Yorkshire. It's near Haworth. Where the Brontës lived. They wrote books."

"Haworth!" I know where the bloody Brontës lived, and what they got up to. I've read all their novels God knows how many times, and I know Yorkshire is up in the north of England somewhere. How far up north?

Not too far, actually. I dump the London A–Z and start rifling through my mental UK atlas. I have a photographic memory for maps, as well as pretty much everything else I see or read, so I can visualise it perfectly and I know exactly where Haworth is. And what it's like—I have a mental image of a *Wuthering Heights* rolling moorland scene. Windswept, dramatic wilderness. These images rush through my head as all goes quiet on the other end. Natasha wisely gives me a moment to collect my scattered wits.

"But I'm in London." Stating the obvious is one of my many talents. I'm in North London, admittedly, but Yorkshire, Haworth, is still two hundred miles away. "How am I supposed to get there ready to start work tomorrow at nine? Which station do the trains to Haworth go from?"

"King's Cross, change at Leeds, then again probably, not really sure…" Always helpful and well-informed, our Natasha. "But the job's not in Haworth. It's in Oakworth and that's another train ride on top, assuming there's a station there. These places up north can be a bit cut off, you know. The train's no good — you'll have to drive up. You could be there in four hours. Five tops."

No station? What sort of place is this? And I happen to know she's wrong. Haworth does have a station, and so does Oakworth. I must have read about this once, because I know that they are on the Worth Valley line and that quaint little steam trains run along there every weekend, full of Thomas the Tank Engine groupies and railway enthusiasts, no doubt. Not much good to me now, though. I need a high-speed rail link or, better still, a helicopter, not the timeless magic of steam.

I glance at my bedside clock. It's just turned seven now, so even if I can set off within half an hour that means arriving in a strange mainline-stationless town after midnight, finding a hotel — if they have one — getting checked in and settled, and up in the morning in time to find this Black Combe place before nine in the morning. Bloody hell.

Even while I'm panicking quietly to myself, though, I know I'm going.

"No need for a hotel." Is Natasha a mind reader now, or did I say all that out loud? "The job is live-in. You'd get all expenses and accommodation, and a tuition fee on top. Shall I tell them you're on your way?"

Pushing all unhelpful irrelevancies out of my head — for example, if I felt like being really picky, I could ask Natasha why anybody would need a live-in music tutor — I jump into action. Too right, I'm on my way. Natasha promises to make the call and I leap out of bed to chuck a few clothes in my holdall and grab my violin. I'm going to Yorkshire.

* * * *

Since my hasty exit from the dreaming spires of Oxford six weeks ago, I'm going out of my mind with boredom. I can't stand it. The last few weeks of bunking up with my mother have been just barely bearable. She means well, I know she loves me, but she always worries about me and my future. She desperately wants me to be safe and settled, but can't for the life of her understand what mental aberration made me dump a distinctly promising career in academia — at one of the most prestigious colleges in the world — and show up on her doorstep without warning, rhyme or reason.

I tried to pass it all off as something fairly casual, told her that I'd seen enough pomposity and pretentiousness at St Hilda's venerable College to last me as many lifetimes as I might be blessed with, and I am desperately longing for a slice of real life. I appreciated it didn't sound convincing, even to me, though I happen to know it's true. Well, some of it. As far as that story goes.

But by the look on her face I had apparently lapsed into some obscure dialect of Swahili — one language I am not especially familiar with — for all the sense I was making. I don't think I was able to articulate my present dilemma very well — unusual for me, I'm normally a precise and persuasive communicator, probably because I usually have the advantage of knowing what I'm talking about. But for once, I don't. I have no idea where the sudden and overwhelming panic came from that drove me to pack in a perfectly nice and well-paid job, a job promising me academic prestige and offering glittering prospects, and present myself instead on her doorstep.

It started weeks, maybe months ago. I was suffocating at Oxford. At first it was just a feeling of inadequacy. Me — inadequate! I couldn't work out where it was all coming from. I'm bloody good at what I do. Used to do. My perfectly logical brain told me there was absolutely no reason to doubt myself. But the doubts still grew. They grew into fear, then into panic attacks. I started forgetting things — appointments, names, deadlines. I started arriving late at work with no idea why or how I got delayed. I was losing track of time. And some days I didn't turn up at all, just stayed under my duvet and ignored my phone as it rang and rang. All the time I was becoming more frightened, more confused.

My memory is exceptional. Truly, truly exceptional. My attention to detail is outstanding. I had no idea what was happening to me. My life, I suppose, was generally crap enough and tedious much of the time, but at least I had my work and I was proud of what I'd achieved in so short a time. Without that, I had nothing. Was nothing.

My team leader and mentor, Professor Benson, spotted that I was slipping up, losing my grip. He commented on it. He was kind, concerned. He said that I looked ill and tired, told me to take some time off. I said I was fine, so he insisted. Ordered me home for a fortnight to rest, recharge. Big mistake. Big, big mistake,

I spent my enforced holiday perched on the end of my lonely little single bed, in my tiny flat on the outskirts of Oxford, eating next to nothing apart from the occasional Pot Noodle, and sleeping for no more than an hour or so at a time. I was turning over and over in my head all the things that were wrong, all the things I didn't believe I could do anymore, all the ways I was letting myself and everyone around me down. Even small, simple tasks became huge, insurmountable problems, and planning anything was completely beyond me. I even found myself sticking Post-it notes on the fridge one day to remind me to put the bin out on the following Tuesday, desperately afraid of the dire consequences that would surely follow if I missed that crucial deadline.

And all that fortnight, the monstrous spectre of my return to the college loomed closer. I counted down the days, then the hours, my panic mounting, my desperation gripping me so fiercely at times that I couldn't breathe.

I started to have asthma attacks—a problem I'd thought I left behind in childhood. I managed to scrounge some Ventolin from the girl in the flat below, saying I'd just run out, when in reality making a doctor's appointment to get a prescription was beyond me. It was a pity, really. A doctor was probably exactly what I needed, though I would never have admitted that to myself. Not then.

I sat in my flat and imagined myself in a cell awaiting execution, conscious of every passing moment, trying to hold onto each second as it slipped inexorably past me and out of my reach. I spent the night before I was due back at work crouched on the floor in my bathroom, shivering. By the time I could put off the evil moment no longer, I was numb with fear. I'd rather have stuck pins in my eyes than go to the college and face a day at work. Worried about being late again, I left my flat about two hours early, determined to walk to the college and clear my head on the way.

I might as well have tried to remove my own spleen with a knife and fork and a couple of aspirins. It just wasn't happening, and by the time I arrived at the college I was little short of sleep-walking, forcing one foot in front of the other by sheer willpower. My all-consuming panic couldn't have been any more compelling if there really had been a pillow over my head, because that was how it felt to me. I was gripped by utter terror and absolute desperation to escape.

That morning is something of a blur now, but I vaguely remember that I made my way on autopilot to the small office I shared with two postgraduates and sat down at my cluttered desk. It was all just as I'd left it, and all the more terrifying for that. Everything that had so scared me before my enforced leave was all still there, waiting for me. Only one of my colleagues was in residence, and Susie's cheery 'hello' only served to prove to me how mentally mashed up I was. I couldn't even remember what the right response was, so I just ignored her, sat down and pressed the button on the front of my PC to fire it up.

"Are you okay? Eva?" The disembodied voice from somewhere nearby eventually penetrated my consciousness and I turned to look. Susie was there, standing just behind me. So was Professor Benson—Ben to us—and they both looked worried, perplexed. Ben stepped forward, reached out for me, and I thought he was going to put his hand on my shoulder. I leapt to my feet, my every confused instinct screaming at me to run for the door. But they were blocking my way. I was trapped. I caught sight of the clock on the wall—nine-forty—and realised I'd been sitting, staring at the blank screen, for over half an hour. I suppose Susie had noticed, become concerned—no flies on that girl—and had gone to fetch the professor. Their sympathetic concern was the final nail in the coffin of my flimsy composure, and I had no other thought in my head by then but to get out of there—just make a run for it and never come back.

So that was exactly what I did. I picked up my bag, went to put my coat on and only then realised I'd never even taken it off. I asked them politely to excuse me, and I left the room. Slowly and calmly, I made my way along the corridor, heading for the outside, and only started to run as though my life depended on it when I hit the fresh air.

Looking back, I know now that I had some sort of mini breakdown. Or maybe not so mini. Nothing else explains my overwhelming desperation, my phobic need to get out of there, to fight my way out if need be and to make my escape. Maybe I should have presented myself at the university health centre. They might have cured me. But instead I went back to my poky little flat, sent an email from my phone resigning my fellowship in the Faculty of Linguistics, apologised to Ben for letting him down, then got in my car and headed for my mother's apartment in North London.

She was delighted to see me at first, thinking I'd come for a little flying surprise visit. Her joy was short-lived. She was as horrified as Ben had been when I told her I'd resigned and was staying. Indefinitely.

Ben was on the phone constantly, talking to my mother because I flatly refused to take his calls. Through her, I learned that he understood—which was more than I could say for me. That he knew I needed more time off, and he thought maybe I should go and have a chat with my GP, but I was not to come back until I felt well enough. Through my mother, I asked him what part of 'I resign' was not perfectly clear to him, and refused to take part in any further discussion.

Despite my mother's pleading, I flatly refused to go anywhere near a doctor either. I knew something was wrong with me, badly wrong, but the last thing I needed—or so I thought, was to be labelled unstable. I knew what they'd have to say. The talk would be of mental health issues. Depression. The very words terrified me, left me feeling weak and inadequate, somehow tainted, and I was having none of that.

So it was just me, my duvet and my mother's home cooking, and for the next four weeks or so that was all my world consisted of. It was enough, and eventually I began to peep out. I began to think it might be safe to actually *come* out, just briefly. I could always scuttle back if things went wrong. What those 'things' might be, I wasn't sure, but the very thought of them scared me rigid. And the first few times I did scuttle back, but eventually I got a bit braver, and began to think maybe I might like to do something after all. I wasn't sure what, as long as it wasn't too challenging. As long as I didn't have problems to solve, new systems to create. I wasn't sure where I wanted to be—as long as it wasn't St Hilda's College, the scene of my terrifying humiliation. I just knew that if I ever, ever had to return there I'd be dragged back down into that dark and terrifying place, and maybe I'd never manage to scramble out again.

So one day, seized by a rare excess of forward-looking enthusiasm, I sauntered into Natasha's pristine agency and told her cockily that I could teach music. And despite her obvious disdain she apparently believed me. What's more, she now seems desperate enough to give me a chance. And I'm desperate enough to take it.

I need to *do something*. I need to be somewhere different, doing something new. Most of all, I need a job. A real job with wages and a contract and a job description, where you have to turn up on time. A job where you need qualifications and actually use them. I need to Do Something Useful. In the real world. Just for once.

Brontë country sounds lovely, on reflection…

Chapter Two

So that's how me, Ludwig and Miranda—my 1990 red Mini with the red, white and blue Union flag criss-crossing the roof—came to be splashing up the M1, torrential rain lashing against the windscreen that has developed a leak, blinded by spray and not able to get above about fifty miles an hour. I have thrown together a bag of just a few essentials and slung it on the back seat, along with my violin, lovingly packed in my chiffon skirt. As Natasha brightly noted, I can always drive back down to London at the weekend to pack properly.

I charged out of my mother's house in Stamford Hill by just turned seven-thirty p.m. I'd never have made it if it hadn't been my mother's night for hitting Covent Garden with her friends from the North London Ladies' Circle. God knows how I'm going to get past her at the weekend to collect any more stuff. I left a quick note to explain, and she's got my mobile number so she can unleash the budgie on me when she gets back and finds me gone. I'm expecting the call before midnight, by which time—roadworks and torrential rain permitting—Miranda and I will be in Yorkshire. Natasha has called the client to tell them I'm on my way, so they're expecting me.

That's a nice feeling, I note with some interest. *To be expected...*

Well, they're expecting someone. Probably not someone quite like me, if I'm totally honest with myself, some scruffy individual in my signature outfit of faded denim jeans, black T-shirt and a hoodie of indeterminate colour but probably grey, turning up on their doorstep in the middle of the night. What was that about first impressions? Did I learn nothing from Natasha? They'll probably set the dogs on me. I could have thought this through a bit better, smartened myself up a bit, even if I was in a rush to get away before my mother got back.

I did remember to bring my certificate proving I hold a BMus from King's College, London, though, so at least they'll know I'm qualified to teach the violin. *And the rest...*

I pass Sheffield at eleven o'clock after a brief stop at a brightly lit motorway services for a burger and a fix of strong coffee. I reach the outskirts of Leeds by half past, and join the M62. A few miles west, I see brown tourist signs announcing the vicinity of the Brontë attractions and head obediently up the M606, an odd little three-mile stretch of motorway that seems to finish up in a field. Then the satnav comes into its own, guiding me through the suburban fringes of Bradford—not too salubrious—onto the ring road, then out again into the open countryside.

Haworth is well signposted, and despite the teeming rain I reach it by around half past midnight. After driving past the quaint little lovingly restored station—*I told you so, Natasha!*—I make my way up the steep and winding main road. I bypass the cobbled, touristy bit of the village, which is silent and deserted at this time, but looks intriguing from what I can see of the little curiosity shops and cafes. Names like Heathcliff's Antique Books and Branwell's Tea Room are just visible through the lashing rain. I make a mental note to come back in daylight for a proper look. When it's dry.

Haworth soon disappears behind me, along with any form of street lighting and other signs of civilisation. I plough on through the pitch-black night. Miranda is still gamely climbing like a mountain goat, and I am secretly relieved that she's made it this far. I don't usually trouble her for more than short jaunts around the city, so this is a big deal for both of us. Although I can't see much around me — visibility is down to around five yards or so — I have a strong sense of space and height. My straight beam points straight up, so I turn that off and settle for the dipped headlights. These last few miles are slow going.

About twenty minutes out of Haworth, I take a right turn as the satnav sends me up a narrow side road. I think we must be somewhere near now but still the satnav wants to continue on. I check. According to the figures on the screen, we have another two and a half miles before we reach our destination. We carry on, down to a slow crawl now because I am terrified of going off the road — if you can call this cart track a road — or clipping one of the dry stone walls on either side.

Onwards, onwards, up the single-track lane, which is now reduced to a muddy, narrow cart track. This can't be right. It's absolutely pitch black everywhere around. The rain has eased a little, maybe, but I can't make out a thing in front of me. The silence is crushing, terrifying. I hadn't realised what a city girl I was. Even if I wanted to turn back—and I do at this moment—there is no space for such an ambitious manoeuvre, even for a tiny car like Miranda. I'm terrified of coming off the road, ending up in a ditch or over a cliff. Or in a river. Or whatever is beyond the pool of light from my headlamps.

Down to about ten miles an hour, and with loyal Ludwig turned down low so I can concentrate, I edge along the track, peering out of the side windows for any sign of life—lights, a house, another vehicle. I see only blackness.

Then I hit something.

My nose pressed to the windscreen, I squint out. It's a gate. A big metal monster of a gate securely hinged to two massive stone pillars, at least seven feet tall. Not a gate to be messed with. *Holy fuck, how did I not see that? It's probably visible from the Moon.*

Should have kept my eyes front—there's a lot to be said for looking where you're going, especially when driving. My mother is always on about it. It's lucky I was going so slow. I only rattled the monster gate—not to mention myself and Miranda's bumper. But this has to be the end of the road. Bloody satnav has got me lost, and stuck up a dead end in the middle of nowhere. There's no room to turn around and it's about five miles to reverse back out. There's nothing but wilderness and dry stone walls for miles around, I've been driving for hours, I've a new job lined up that I can't find… I'm dead tired, scared and probably about to cry.

Terrified of the silence and the blackness, I grab my hoodie from the back seat, slip my arms through and pull the hood up over my head. Why didn't I think to bring a raincoat? I climb out to check how close I am to the ditch and try to work out if a three — *who am I kidding? Thirty-three* — point turn might be feasible.

With a smooth whirr, the gate starts to open. Bloody hell, it must be one of those electric things with a sensor. It knows I'm here. It's letting me in. There must be someone about, and if there is I can find out where I am and where this Black Combe place is. I'm saved!

On that joyous thought, I suddenly catch sight of bright lights hurtling towards me from out of the darkness back along the lane, and they are coming up fast. I hear the growling purr of a powerful engine as a big, long, low black car comes into view round the final bend. From the brief glance I get, I know it's one of those hideously expensive, gas-guzzling, penis-substitute boy's toys — quite beautiful, really, if you like that sort of thing.

There's a momentary lurch as the driver spots Miranda at the last moment and tries to brake. *Not a chance.*

From my vantage point by Miranda's front bumper — miraculously unblemished by the recent encounter with the gate from hell — I hear the scream of tyres desperately trying to grab wet tarmac, then the harsh crash of impact as the prick-mobile roars straight into the back of my faithful little Mini. As I leap for my life the momentum takes both cars forward, through the now wide-open gate, onto a gravel driveway beyond, where they both stop.

And after the clattering racket of grating metal comes a hush, the only sound now good old Ludwig, who is still gently pouring forth from my CD player. I note idly that we've now reached the final movement of his Symphony Number 9 in D minor — 'Ode to Joy'. *Perfect!*

Disentangling myself from my relatively safe refuge behind the massive stone gatepost, I creep forward to survey the damage. At first sight, the gas-guzzling monster looks to have come off worst, so apparently there is some justice in this world. There's steam coming from under its bonnet—which is not exactly straight and sleek anymore—and some liquid dribbling underneath. In contrast Miranda looks quite chipper, considering. A couple more dents and scratches on her rear end, which are clearly shown up by one searchlight still functioning on the front of her attacker, but she'll live. Probably.

Then all hell breaks loose.

The driver's door of the gas-guzzler flies open. "What the fuck is that wreck doing there?"

The man who storms out is tall, broad-shouldered, spitting with fury—and absolutely beautiful. I am stunned and can only stare. I think my mouth is open. I fumble in my hoodie pocket for my glasses.

His long, dark hair—quickly drenched in the continuing downpour—is thick, wavy and brushes his collar. He is smartly dressed in a crisp white shirt, open at the neck with no tie, and charcoal-grey trousers. Reaching back into his car, he grabs a leather bomber jacket and thrusts his arms into the sleeves, then zips it up and pulls the collar up around his neck. His obviously expensive clothes look completely incongruous out here in the wilds of the Yorkshire moorland, and that jacket is probably never going to recover from the soaking it's getting. But he's incandescent with rage and obviously not thinking of his wardrobe at this precise moment. I manage to spot highly polished Italian leather shoes. Wellies would have been more practical…

He is towering over Miranda, looking as if he might just pick her up and lob her back out through the gate.

I have never seen a man I've thought beautiful before, but there is no other way to describe him. I stand there, dripping wet and just gaping. After a few moments, I realise he hasn't seen me yet. His outrage would be comical if he wasn't so intimidating, his gaze going from his crumpled bonnet to Miranda's relatively unscathed rear end and back, and his fingers combing roughly through his hair. He bends to look into Miranda's driving seat, then stands back, obviously puzzled. Leaning down again, he reaches in and turns off the engine, and Ludwig finally quietens. He pockets my car keys, then straightens to look around him, clearly puzzled. *Uh-oh, time to make myself known.* "Are you all right?"

At my question, he whirls and — by the look of total amazement on his face — he can't believe what's in front of him. And I know what he's thinking. I've seen that look before. Frequently. All he sees is what appears to be a scruffy teenager in a hoodie, faded jeans and trainers, soaking wet. Probably joyriding in a stolen car, and definitely up to no good on his quiet country lane in the dead of night.

Damage limitation seems called for. I walk up to him, hand outstretched, my face plastered with the politest smile I can manage. "Good evening. Sorry about that. I'm Eva Byrne. I'm afraid I'm not familiar with this area. I'm trying to find a place called Black Combe and I seem to have taken a wrong turn somewhere. I wonder if you can direct me?"

He looks at me, then at my hand — checking for hidden flick-knives? — then back at my face. Then good manners take over, just momentarily, because he takes my hand briefly and shakes it before stepping away to more closely inspect the damage to his penis substitute. He walks slowly around his once-gorgeous car, crouching to examine the crumpled bonnet and smashed headlamp, and God knows what other internal injuries, judging by all the steam and fluid slopping about.

Finally standing upright again and towering over me—he is nearly a foot taller than I am—he glowers over my head in the direction of poor, innocent Miranda. "Is this heap of junk yours, or did you steal it?"

I *knew* that was what he was thinking and suddenly—maybe it's the stress, or delayed shock or something—I start to lose my cool. I don't see why I should take that sort of shit, even if he is a bit upset and his penis—*I mean, car*—has got bent.

"Yes, it's mine. And it's in better shape than yours looks to be just at this moment, you maniac!"

Ignoring my comment, he launches into another attack. His brief flirtation with good manners at an end, he marches over to Miranda and kicks her back wheel, scuffing his lovely shoe. "What the fucking hell were you doing dumping that pile of shite in front of my gate? In fact, what the hell are you doing up here anyway, Miss...Byrne?"

"I told you already, Mr...?" As he's not offering to introduce himself properly, I think it best to remind him of my predicament. "I'm looking for Black Combe..."

"Well, you've found it all right. What I want to know is why you were barricading my gate?"

"It was a dead end, or so I thought, so I stopped to work out what to do next, and suddenly you came tearing up the road and crashed right into Miranda. You should have been looking where you were going, you moron. And you were driving too fast in this rain. Have you read the Highway Code recently? Have you heard of stopping distances? You could have killed me..."

As that possibility sinks in I suddenly start to feel a bit weak at the knees. It had been a narrow escape. What if I'd been standing behind Miranda instead of to the side? I would have been splattered all over the front of that bloody racing car. I think I'm going to be sick. Correction, I *know* I am. Very soon.

His car is nearest to me and I lean against it, taking deep breaths and bending at the waist as I feel my stomach starting to heave. Mr Beautiful-When-He's-Angry is suddenly alongside me. My eyes fixed on the ground, I can see his shiny shoes, one of them scuffed from his unprovoked attack on Miranda, and all I can think of is how mortifying it will be to splatter them with the contents of my stomach. God, this is all I need to top off the journey from hell — throwing up all over a perfect stranger.

Then it's all out of my hands — or more accurately out of my stomach — as I heave up my guts down the prick-mobile's driver's door.

"Jesus." I can hear his muttered curse, but the next thing I know he has produced a clean handkerchief — the proper fabric sort that you have to wash and iron — and he hands it to me. "Here, wipe your mouth." Then he snaps the top off a small bottle of water and hands that to me too. "Rinse."

I am happy to oblige, starting to feel a bit steadier, but as my mind once again takes over control of my bodily functions, the depth of my humiliation starts to sink in. The only saving grace is that the rain is washing my vomit from the car door, and it is trickling away down the lane.

'My gate.' He said 'my gate'.

Somehow through all the nausea, throwing up, and Biblical rain I have registered that this seems to be Black Combe — *sorry satnav, I should have had more faith* — and that it is *his* property. I know there must be other instances of people having been fired before they even start work, but do they usually wreck their employer's car, then throw up on it? This must be some sort of record.

Suddenly the rain stops, and I realise Mr Beautiful has produced a large golf umbrella from somewhere — I assume his car boot — and he is holding it over both of us. He looks down at me in distaste and I realise I can't really blame him. I offer him his hanky back, and his raised palm and quick headshake make it clear he'd rather I kept it to myself.

"Again, what the hell are you doing here?" He's moderated his voice to aggrieved exasperation now, but he clearly wants an answer.

"I'm the new music teacher."

"What?"

"The new music teacher. From Little Maestros."

"Little…?"

"I teach violin. You want a violin tutor. You said they had to send someone by tomorrow. So here I am. Today."

"You're Rosie's new violin tutor? What's wrong with turning up in broad daylight, for God's sake? Do you know what time it is?"

"I've come a long way. I didn't want to be late."

"You call this not being late? It's one in the morning. Bloody fucking hell!" Incredulous, and looking me up and down with a mixture of distaste and disbelief, I can tell he is starting to itemise all the potentially disastrous implications of letting some little scruff come into his no doubt pristine and perfect home, masquerading as a music teacher. "Are you even qualified?"

Now this I had been expecting, and I'm ready. Pushing past him to reach into Miranda's back seat, I pull out my holdall — which contains mainly the few clothes I threw together what seems like a lifetime ago, back in my room in my mother's house in London, when everything was sane and normal and dry — and start rummaging around. Grabbing the bunch of documents I shoved in there, I start to rifle through a file of soggy paperwork. Finding my BMus certificate, I thrust it under his nose, hoping he won't want to examine it too closely because if he does he is sure to query the date. I attempt to divert his attention with more paperwork. "There, that proves it. Do you want proof of ID, just in case it's a fake?" I haven't forgotten Natasha's doubts, so I shove another crumpled piece of wet paper at him, my birth certificate this time, verifying my advanced age of twenty-two. "And I've got a violin in there too." I jerk my thumb back towards Miranda. "Want a demonstration?"

"Too right I want a bloody demonstration, but not out here. I'm already piss-wet through."

Tell me about it. I know it's bloody raining. Does he think I'm totally blind? On reflection, better not to mention that I managed to drive straight into his not exactly invisible gate just before he came hurtling up the lane.

"Come on, let's take this inside."

Deliberately ignoring my outstretched hand as I wait for him to return my certificates, he tucks my precious papers into the inside pocket of his jacket and picks up my holdall. Still grasping the brolly, he gestures for me to follow him. Stretching once more across Miranda's back seat, I grab my battered violin case, then trot to catch him up as he strides off into the darkness. We crunch across the gravel together, me following him and trying to keep up with the umbrella. His sharp tone suggests his temper hasn't cooled much, but I note that, somehow, he smells wonderful. And he seems inclined to offer me shelter, at least temporarily.

He obviously knows where he is headed and I have to break into a trot every few yards to keep up with his long strides. About thirty seconds later the house comes into view. I can't see much detail through the rain but it is obviously big, solidly built of dark Yorkshire stone, and old. Three large, wide stone slabs make up the entrance steps, topped by a dark wooden door with iron studs sticking out of its surface.

Pulling a key from his trouser pocket, he opens the door before stepping back and gesturing me past him. I slip inside gratefully to find myself dripping onto the tiled floor of a brightly lit entrance hallway. Facing me is a wide wooden staircase with a beautifully carved banister whose shine rivals my companion's Italian shoes. I glance furtively down at those, checking for any lingering signs of my vomit in the light. No, still clean and shiny. Relief!

I deposit my violin case on the floor by my feet and look around me as my companion closes the door, then shucks out of his soaked leather jacket. He gives it a shake and droplets of water scatter around the hallway, and I hear him muttering something along the lines of "…bloody fucking ruined…" as he dumps it over the banister at the bottom of the stairs. I start to wonder if I can sneak my certificates back out of his pocket while he's not looking, but even as I turn that possibility over in my mind he retrieves them himself. He looks properly at them now, in the light. Thankfully, he is more interested in my birth certificate than the degree.

"Evangelica—now that's a name to grow into..." He looks at me, his eyes raking up and down my admittedly small frame, his gaze distinctly derisive.

"Yes. I was named after my grandmother." *Why tell him that? He's not interested in my family history. Stop babbling, fool.*

"What's she like?"

"Who?"

"Evangelica the First, your grandmother. Do you take after her?"

"I don't know. She died before I was born. And my dad died when I was seven, so he didn't tell me that much about her either. I don't think my mother knew her that well. She played the piano..." I trail off, realising he probably didn't mean for me to provide my entire life story. "Anyway, it's Eva. Or Miss Byrne when I'm teaching."

He grins sardonically, obviously less than impressed at my attempt to establish some degree of authority and seriousness despite my unpromising first impression. *Sarcastic bastard!*

He goes on, still clearly intent on putting me down at any and every opportunity. I feel myself start to bristle. Who the hell does he think he is? *He's your new employer, and you need this job, so keep it civil.*

"So that's where your alleged musical talent came from then, I daresay. I'm looking forward to seeing whether the lovely Evangelica the First had her name wasted on you."

He doesn't wait for me to reply, probably fortunate for me, as I suspect my response would not have been calculated to endear me to my new boss. He shoves my precious papers back into his jacket pocket before yelling down the corridor leading away from the front door, towards the rear of the house. "Grace, are you still up? It's me."

There is a staircase right in front of us, and on either side are closed doors, painted a smart, bright white, obviously leading to the front reception rooms. I hear a door open and shut somewhere at the back of the house, behind the staircase, then pandemonium breaks loose as what appears to be a small pony hurtles down the corridor and launches itself at my companion. Raising one magic, powerful, authoritative finger, my new employer stops the headlong dash and the pony drops into a sit at his feet.

Now I see that the huge black and brown blur is in fact the largest and woolliest dog I think I've ever seen, and the huge tail thumping the floor suggests it is very pleased to see my companion. It ignores me totally, its adoring eyes riveted on its master.

By way of acknowledgement, he makes a clicking noise with his tongue and reaches down to tug the dog's ears. "Hello, Barney. How goes it, mate? Pleased to see me?"

By way of answer, the dog thumps its tail faster, harder as it shuffles closer to my companion and rubs its massive head against his thigh.

I am shocked to find myself harbouring the unfamiliar notion that snuggling up to this man could be an interesting idea. Christ, where did that come from? I've never had the least inclination to snuggle up to any man in my life. Never! And just because this one might be the most attractive example I've ever come across as far as I can recall—and I do have perfect recall—that doesn't change the fact that he's also grumpy, sneering and plain unpleasant. I don't even like him, so I can't possibly be attracted to him.

As I am trying to sort this tangle out in my head and failing to make sense of any of it, another whirlwind comes rushing in from the back of the house, this time in the form of a small, blonde-haired woman, aged—I'd guess—around fifty-five. Her bow wave of questions arrives momentarily before she does.

"Mr Darke, is that you? I didn't expect to see you tonight. I thought you were in Leeds until Friday. How've you got here? And what are you doing coming in the front? I didn't hear your car. Lord, you're soaking..."

Suddenly, as she spots me dripping all over her floor as well, her face lights up in the warmest smile I've seen in rather a long time.

Dropping all interest in my surly host and turning her attention to me, she rushes on. "Ah, luvvie, you must be Miss Byrne. I was getting that worried about you—I was expecting you ages ago and I thought you must have got lost in all this rain, and it's awful out there tonight." She stops briefly to catch a breath, then launches back into her flow before either of us can offer any sort of response. "What a good thing you found her, Mr Darke. She might have been wandering about out there all night. Oh, bless you, love, you're drenched! You'll be catching your death. Here, give me your top and I'll stick it on the radiator. Mr Darke, have we got any dry clothes for the poor child?"

She holds her hand outstretched, waiting for my hoodie, and it never occurs to me to argue. I unzip it, push the hood back off my face and shrug out of the sopping fleece without a word, handing it over for whatever remedial treatment this latest force of nature can apply. Released from the confines of the hood my unruly hair, made even wilder by the dampness it has encountered over the last few minutes, bursts out in all its carroty glory, a mass of spiralling tendrils around my face and dripping down my back. I try ineffectually to push it back behind my ears but, as ever, it has a life of its own and other plans. Realising I still have my glasses perched on my nose, I reach for the pocket of my hoodie before it is borne away by the whirlwind, grabbing my glasses case and shoving my specs in before jamming it into the pocket of my jeans.

I can feel 'Mr Darke' looking at me and realise — again to my surprise, because these things don't normally bother me at all — that I am cringing, embarrassed to my core, acutely aware of my unprepossessing appearance under this mop of ginger chaos, and the pathetically soggy picture I must be presenting. First impressions, Christ! Can this get any worse?

Previously hidden under my hoodie, my outfit is less than impressive. I am wearing a plain black, short-sleeved T-shirt, modestly round-necked and just about long enough to reach the waistband of my jeans as long as I don't try to reach up for anything. I didn't bother with a bra when I threw my clothes on after Natasha's call a lifetime ago, so my miniscule breasts are just sitting there looking ridiculous, especially as my nipples are standing to attention from the rain and wind-chill. I realise I am shivering, mostly from cold but probably not entirely.

He stares at me, looking me up and down, and despite — or maybe because of — his particular interest in my protruding nipples, he obviously finds me wanting. I raise my chin, defiant and not about to apologise for myself again, but at the same time wishing I could have managed to impress him. Just a little bit. Suddenly, his good opinion matters to me...

"Lord, she's shivering. Come on through, love, and let's get you warmed up. Pretty hair, by the way..." My hoodie and the whirlwind start off back along the corridor heading towards the bowels of the house. I start after them.

"Seems you are expected after all. And aren't you forgetting something?" I turn to see him nod towards my violin case, still on the floor by the door. "You'll be needing that."

After picking the case up by the handle, I step past him to follow my hoodie along the corridor and into a huge kitchen at the back of the house, one very grumpy Mr Darke and one big, very delighted black dog trooping along behind me.

The kitchen is a lovely, homey mix of old and new, traditional and ultra-modern. The floor is gorgeous, flagged with Yorkshire stone, the whole room dominated by a huge oak table, around which six solid-looking oak chairs are scattered. A large Aga sits in the fireplace, a bright red kettle hissing gently on top of it alongside some sort of lidded casserole dish, and a fluffy blanket on the floor next to it indicates where Barney likes to spend his downtime. He pads in after me and flops down in his bed.

Two walls are lined with modern, fitted units and I notice a large window over the sink, roller blind pulled down now against the drizzling night sky. A huge, American-style double-door refrigerator occupies another wall, opposite the Aga, and Mr Darke strolls over to it. Opening one of the doors, he reaches in for a large carton of fresh orange juice and drinks straight from the neck. He then replaces the carton and leans back against the closed fridge door to regard me coldly.

Before he can speak again, the whirlwind takes charge. "I'm Grace—Mrs Richardson," she begins. "I generally look after things here. Cooking, seeing to the housekeeping, looking after little Rosie—whatever needs doing, really."

"Hello, I'm very pleased to meet you, Mrs Richardson." Still clutching my violin case with my left hand, I hold out the right one, pleased to be able to demonstrate some semblance of social grace. She shakes it warmly.

Encouraged, I try again with *him*. "And you too, Mr Darke. We couldn't really introduce ourselves properly outside." I offer him my hand to shake again, and he takes it, nodding slightly in acknowledgement. Now's my chance to tell my side of it, explain what the hell I'm doing showing up at this time of night, and I'm not letting anyone stop me.

"I'm Eva Byrne. My agency, Little Maestros, contacted me to ask if I could take over as music tutor here, do Rosie's violin lessons whilst your normal teacher is laid up. It was very short notice, I'm afraid. I only got the phone call late this afternoon and I got here as soon as I could, but with the weather... And it's a long way up here from London, so I'm afraid it's very late. I really am sorry to have inconvenienced you like this..."

"You drove all the way here from London, in that leaking, clapped out old rot-bucket you dumped down by my gate?" Ah, clearly Miranda's charms are lost on this Philistine... "You're lucky to have got this far in one piece."

"Is there a problem down by the gate?" Mrs Richardson is looking puzzled and slightly concerned.

"Don't ask," he says curtly, and turns to me. "Let's see if you really can play that thing."

"Yes, of course…" I place the violin case on the floor and start to unzip it.

"Oh, a tune will be lovely, but not until she's had a bite to eat and got warmed up." Mrs Richardson is determined to nourish and nurture me, it seems. I am incredibly grateful, actually, because the truth is I am chilled to the bone and famished. "I hope you like lamb hotpot—I saved you some and it's been keeping nice and hot here." She lifts the lid on the casserole and gives it a stir with a large spoon. "Should warm you up a treat. Oh, you're not a vegetarian, are you?" She glances at me, as if worried I might have some more funny habits, on top of arriving in perfect stranger's kitchen at one in the morning.

"No, I love lamb hotpot. And I'm starving. This is very kind of you, really." The delicious smells are wafting around me and I am salivating. I haven't eaten since I grabbed that burger at Woodall Services, south of Sheffield. How soon can I get my hands on a bowlful of that stuff, I wonder?

Pretty much straight away, it seems. Mrs Richardson ladles a generous helping into a brown earthenware bowl and puts it on the table. Even before I can sit down—and I'm no slouch—it is joined by a spoon and a half loaf of crusty bread on a chunky wooden bread board, a couple of doorsteps already sliced. A lethal-looking breadknife lies alongside the loaf, ready to do further damage as required.

"What about you, Mr Darke? There's plenty…"

"I don't think I've ever turned down your hotpot, Grace," he says, taking the chair opposite mine and reaching for the breadknife.

After placing another full, steaming bowl in front of him and passing him a spoon, Mrs Richardson sits at the end of the table, looking from Mr Darke to me and back again, obviously waiting for an explanation now that the urgent matters of food and warmth seem to be in hand. Neither of us is forthcoming, but she's not put off.

"So, how come you're both so wet?" Turning to her employer she tries a bit of gentle humour. "I know you like to drive with the top down on that Porsche of yours, Mr Darke, but tonight's hardly the right weather for all that malarkey."

The humour is lost on him. It would appear he is just not ready to see the funny side of this—yet.

"I crashed the Porsche. Into Miss Byrne's"—he hesitates, lost for a word to accurately describe the contemptible object he clearly considers Miranda to be—"vehicle"—*well, I suppose that will do*—"which was dumped in my gateway. I activated the gate from my remote"—*ah, that explains the mysteriously opening gate just before he screeched round the bend*—"and piled into the heap of junk Miss Byrne seems to have managed to drag up here from London."

Mrs Richardson is duly horrified. "Oh, you poor dears. Are you both okay? Do you need a doctor?"

He cuts her off with a wave of his hand. "Miss Byrne wasn't actually in her car when I hit it—I'm not sure why…" He glances at me suspiciously, and I open my mouth to start to explain, but he cuts me off. "Later." Turning back to Mrs Richardson, he continues, "No, no medical attention needed. What we will need is a tow truck. I'll sort it first thing."

"Well, thank goodness for that, could have been a lot worse. So you got soaked to the skin just walking up the drive?"

"Yes, pretty much."

He turns his full attention to the hotpot and so do I. There is silence for a few minutes as we both dip bread and shovel the stew into our mouths. Mrs Richardson refills both bowls without asking, and we both nod thankfully at her and stick our noses back in the metaphorical trough.

"More hotpot, Miss Byrne?" asks Mrs Richardson eventually, as my slurping finally slows down.

"No, thanks—but that was wonderful." I am pleasantly full, and even starting to feel warm at last. And suddenly I realise how very tired I am. Glancing at the clock on the wall over the fireplace, I am horrified to see it is two-fifteen. I am supposed to be starting work teaching little Rosie in less than seven hours' time!

"God, is it really that late?" I gasp.

"Yes. Time for your practical," Mr Darke says softly, leaning back in his chair. Stretching out his foot, he pushes my violin case towards me across the kitchen floor. "You promised me a demonstration of your...skills. By way of a job interview. Then we'll decide if you're a music teacher or not."

Tired as I am, I know I can handle this. This is my moment. Without a word, I kneel by the violin case and carefully open the lid, then extract the instrument from among the folds of my chiffon skirt. Unclipping the bow from the lid of the case, I stand up. I draw the bow experimentally along the strings, just to hear the tone and make any minor tuning adjustments. I have a good ear, and with only minute twists of the keys on the neck of the violin it is perfect, ready to play.

"Any requests?" I ask.

"No, you choose." He is still seated at the table, waiting. And apparently not expecting much.

Mrs Richardson has been bustling around the sink, clearing up after our meal, but she also comes to sit back down, drying her hands. Even Barney has opened one of his eyes. All three settle themselves, watching me.

Stepping slightly farther back, away from the table, I stand facing my audience with the door open behind me. I place the violin under my chin, resting my face against it like a favourite pillow, and draw in one long breath. I let it out slowly, and again. My feet are planted firmly, about a foot apart. I am centred, grounded. In my element. Now, at least, this I *am* good at.

Leaning into the violin and closing my eyes, I start one of my favourite melodies, not really written for violin—but I think it works beautifully and I love it. The opening, evocative strains of Ravel's 'Boléro' fill the room. I don't need to look up, or hear his sharp intake of breath as he recognises the piece, to know that Mr Darke is stunned. He didn't expect this from me. I am glowing inside because I know, at last, I have him.

I hear a slight noise behind me and open my eyes to see Mr Darke leaning slightly to see around me. Placing his index finger vertically across his mouth, he signals for quiet, then beckons with his hand. A little shadow slips around and past me.

A small girl—impossibly pretty, with long, straight dark hair—runs across the room and climbs onto his knee, and puts her little arms around his neck. She looks sleepy and is wearing a long, pale pink nightie. Her feet are bare. He hugs her, whispers something in her ear that makes her smile, and he kisses her hair. Then they both turn back to me, silent, watching, listening intently as I continue to play.

Completely in my element, absolutely in control of my audience, the music, the instrument, I sway gently as I slowly, surely develop the piece. I build the melody, pouring my own energy into it, louder, faster, ever more compelling as my bow flies back and forth across the resin-heavy horsehair strings. Unerring, every note perfect, I feel the familiar pull of the evocative music and lose myself in it, completely alert but at the same time only dimly aware of my surroundings, my audience. I coax the music towards its crashing crescendo. I am so exhilarated, so pumped up I feel sure I can fly in that moment, but as the final note dies away I am also aware of feeling drained, as if my last dregs of energy were poured into that piece.

No one moves. No one speaks. In the silence that follows, I straighten and stand before them, violin in my left hand and bow in my right, both now pointed down at the floor. Raising my eyes, I meet Mr Darke's gaze.

His face is still, expressionless, but his beautiful dark brown eyes are warm, admiring, the passion of the piece not lost on him. I feel a clenching low down in my belly, glad that I have somehow affected him, touched him. We stare across the kitchen at each other for long moments before he finally comes to his feet, holding the little girl in his arms.

"Bravo, Miss Byrne," he says softly, bowing his head to me. "That was superb."

Mrs Richardson leaps to her feet, finding her voice at last. Clapping wildly, she can't seem to find the right words to express her delight at my impromptu performance in her homey kitchen. "Oh, how wonderful, that was lovely. Really lovely. You should be on the stage, love, you really should. Wasn't that good, Mr Darke? Absolutely beautiful. Do you know any more tunes like that?"

"Yes, I know lots of tunes," I answer quietly.

Turning to the little girl still clinging to Mr Darke's neck and peeking at me through her hair, I think it's time to make friends. "You must be Rosie."

She nods shyly.

"My name is Eva, Eva Byrne. I hear you like to play the violin too, so I am hoping we can play together. Would that be okay?"

Wriggling out of her father's arms, she runs her hand along the edge of the table, looking at her bare feet, not sure yet about me. Peeping up at me through her hair, she decides to risk it. "Can you teach me that tune? The one you just did?"

"Yes, if you like. It sounds even better if two people play it."

"I'm not as good as you."

"I expect I've had more practice."

At last, she smiles up at me. "Do I have to call you Miss Byrne? You're not old like Miss Snow." *Miss Snow?*

"That's Rosie's teacher down at the school. Just retired at the end of the summer term," supplied Mrs Richardson, noticing my puzzled expression, no doubt.

"My first name is Eva. You can use that if it's easier."

"It's Miss Byrne when you're teaching, is it not— Miss Byrne?" Ah, so he hasn't quite finished taking the piss out of me.

"Oh, yes, that's right. Miss Byrne, please." No harm in stamping my authority on the situation, such as it is.

"Hello, Miss Byrne. I'm glad you've come. I tried to stay awake for you, but I had to go to bed. When can we start lessons? I have a violin too." She smiles brilliantly. I know I have made another friend in this place.

"It's time we got Miss Byrne, Evangelica…Eva…into bed." My insides start doing somersaults, even though I know he didn't mean to be suggestive. Well, *maybe* he didn't… Still, I feel myself start to blush. As I glance up at him his eyes are on mine, hot and intent, and I am suddenly not sure his words were accidental.

Stepping in to break the tension, Mrs Richardson comes to my rescue. "I made up a room for Miss Byrne—the guest room at the back, opposite Rosie's. There's a nice view of the moors from that side and I thought she might like it…"

"Good choice." Bending to pick up Rosie, who wraps her legs around his waist as he arranges her on his left hip, Mr Darke strolls towards the door. "I'll show Miss Byrne up, and put this little imp back to bed." He blows a raspberry into Rosie's neck and she giggles, cuddling in tightly to his chest. *Lucky kid.*

Astonished at the disconcerting way my thoughts are unravelling around this rude and beautiful man, I say my 'goodnights' and 'thank you agains' to Mrs Richardson before following him out of the door. He strolls along the corridor back to the bottom of the stairs, where his leather jacket, complete with my precious papers in the inside pocket, is still draped over the banister, dripping. Grabbing the jacket, he shakes it again, then hands it to Rosie.

"Hold that, would you, princess?" With his other hand he reaches down to pick up my holdall, still waiting, forgotten, by the front door.

Making his way up the stairs with Rosie in his arms and me in tow, he looks gentler now, less intimidating. Maybe we could get along together after all. I wish.

At the top of the stairs he strides along the carpeted landing, passing several white-painted doors.

"You can have a proper tour tomorrow, in the daylight," he calls back over his shoulder. "The place is fairly big, but Rosie'll make sure you don't get lost." Not him, then? Maybe he's not staying long and perhaps he won't be here tomorrow. I realise I am saddened by that thought. The place will seem empty without him.

Reaching the end of the landing, he opens the last door on his right and strides in. He flicks the light switch as I follow, to reveal a fairly large and very pretty room. It is decorated in yellow and pale blue, with a deep eggshell blue carpet and white wooden furniture, and the double bed, covered by a dove grey duvet, looks like a dream come true. The floor-length curtains are closed to make it seem even cosier, and fresh flowers have been arranged in a vase on a side table to complete the welcome.

After depositing my holdall on the bed, Mr Darke turns for the door.

"Shower and en suite are over there." He gestures with his head towards the door in the far corner of the room. "Make yourself comfortable and get some sleep. I'll see you tomorrow." *Oh, still intending to be here, then?* "Oh, and don't bother about starting work at nine — we could all do with a lie-in."

"Thank you. Goodnight, Mr Darke. Goodnight, Rosie. And thanks for bringing my bag up."

"You're welcome. And it's Nathan."

"What? What is?"

"Nathan. My name's Nathan."

As I stand staring at him, unaccountably delighted to be on first name terms, he stops in the doorway, a sleeping Rosie now drooping over his shoulder.

"One last thing, Evangelica." He turns to me with a slight smile, his eyes warm now, regarding me closely. "Have you ever worked in a library?"

Chapter Three

I feel great. Fabulous. Refreshed. Vibrant and alive. Eager to... *Eager to what?*

In that hazy space between sleeping and waking, I stretch and roll onto my back, totally content, extending my whole length from headboard to foot of the bed, pointing my toes to ease out the last remaining kinks. I have just slept better than I have in ages, certainly since my escape from St Hilda's. A solid God knows how many hours of deep, uninterrupted sleep, and I'm not sure I really want to surface any time soon. Cracking my eyes slightly, I can tell it's light, but other than that I have no idea what time it is. I'm not sure I care, but out of habit I reach out my right arm, feeling around for my trusty little travel alarm clock. Nothing. No clock, no bedside table, just empty space where my stuff should be.

What the fuck? I open my eyes properly and start to sit up, panicked momentarily by the strangeness, then remembering.

I'm not at home. Was St Hilda's home? Certainly I never thought of it as home. And I'm not at my mother's home. I'm in someone else's home, somewhere in the wilds of Yorkshire where it rains a lot and there are no mainline stations for miles. I lie back down and pull the duvet up to my chin defensively, as the events of yesterday come flooding back. Natasha's call, the endless hours spent driving through torrential rain to the back of beyond, getting lost, Miranda getting pranged by the gorgeous Mr Darke... *No – Nathan, he said to call him Nathan.*

Somehow he doesn't seem like a Nathan, more a Heathcliff or a Mr Rochester, except that that's me being fanciful. I might be a lot of weird things, but fanciful isn't one of them. I give myself one of my self-betterment lectures, along the lines of, *Get a grip. He's your employer, for goodness' sake. Rich, probably, from what I've seen so far of this place. Married possibly, and a father definitely, and he is so not interested in a scruffy little fiddle player like you.*

I cringe inside as I remember making a fool of myself by yelling at him out there in the pouring rain—not that he seemed to notice that, he was too busy slagging me and Miranda off—then throwing up all over his car. Then I went on to make a pig of myself in his cosy kitchen, guzzling lamb hotpot—Christ, I was starving last night. Mind you, the lovely Nathan Darke shifted as much hotpot as I did.

Then came my moment of glory, courtesy of Ravel and his lovely, sensual, atmospheric melody. That moment was sublime and I just know it will live with me forever. I go warm again, lying there tucked under my duvet, basking in the inner glow. I know I am smiling to myself in smug satisfaction, remembering, reliving the silence in the room as I finished playing and looked up, met his eyes and saw...what?

Something certainly that had not been there before. Might have been admiration? Awe? Envy?

Warmth, certainly, and interest. I had his full attention, and for the right reasons at last.

Whatever he may have been thinking, I just know down to my stretched-out toes that I nailed it. I impressed him. It was the performance of my life. I've never played better, technically and with more emotion, than I did last night. I wanted to perform for him. That's what I set out to do and I did it. Perfectly.

It means everything to me and for once I feel so powerful inside. If there's a swimming pool anywhere in this godforsaken outpost, I don't doubt I could walk across it for my encore.

Wide awake now, I see that my pretty blue and yellow guest room is bathed in the watery sunlight slipping in through a crack in the curtains. Probably means it's stopped raining, and come to think I can't hear it lashing against the windows anymore, the way I did last night in those moments before I went comatose. Which was about thirty seconds after my head hit the pillow. I was exhausted—from the drive, certainly, but also from the nervous energy I expended trying to hold onto my equilibrium around Mr Nathan Darke. He is definitely an intimidating individual—an attractive man who knows it, uses it and is used to getting his own way. Certainly he had no hesitation in bossing me around. Bullying me, even, and I start to realise I am not all that comfortable with that thought. It reminds me of being back at school when I was quite little—not fitting in, the butt of some joke I didn't understand, isolated and unsure what to do to, how to belong.

Around him, I realise, I am vulnerable, out of my depth. He makes me nervous, and I am annoyed with myself for letting that happen, for slipping into that mode. I am not a scared little kid anymore and my sensible, grown-up head tells me that my feelings and responses are mine to control, not his. But still.

Nathan has many fine qualities, clearly. I saw some of them last night. His tenderness and obvious love for his daughter, his affection for his dog and his respect for his housekeeper. He reserved his suspicion and contempt, the unreasonable criticism and withering put-downs for me. Without the lovely Mrs Richardson's intervention, I'm still not sure he wouldn't have just slung me back out in the rain. That was, at least, until I played my violin for him. *Yes!*

I push back the duvet and swing my legs out onto the floor. I slept in just a long, baggy T-shirt, which I had remembered to screw up in the bottom of my holdall, and now it swishes around my thighs as I head for the window to check what the weather is doing today. Pulling back the heavy yellow curtain, I gasp. I can only stare in awed silence.

The scenery stretching out before me is absolutely breathtaking. Stunning. I have never seen any place lovelier. Or more austere. My mental image of the Brontë moors didn't remotely do justice to the real thing. As far as I can see, in every direction, lies unbroken, undulating glorious moorland. The colours are vibrant, sparkling, still wet from the previous night's downpour. The near to middle distance is a glittering kaleidoscope of reds, purples, olives, browns, greens and golds as the heather and bracken, grassland and wildflowers blend into one, seeming to move and rotate, still glittering and shiny from the dampness in the air, catching and reflecting the morning sunlight. In the farther distance are soft pale greys, darker smokiness and pale blue smudges of wispy mist circling the higher peaks, a variegated canvas of softly muted beauty. My eye is caught by the glint of light reflecting off water in the bottom of the valley over to my right—a glittering, dark, deep grey, the surface rippling gently in the slight breeze. A lake, perhaps, or maybe a reservoir.

I remember the strong impression of height and distance, and of wide, open vastness surrounding me as Miranda chugged on and up through the inky blackness and driving rain last night. That was no illusion and the sense of limitless space overwhelms me now, as the bright daylight washes over the expansive wildness before me. Even though all this beauty—the colours and textures of this grand and timeless landscape—was invisible to me, I recognised its aura last night. I felt the essence of it all around me then, unseen, and I am drenched in it again now as I open the window and breathe deeply, let it pour in, filling my senses.

It is irresistible, timeless and yet constantly changing as the light and shadows shift, as clouds flit across the sky, interrupting the sunlight as they pass, then releasing it back to fall across the moorland once more in dazzling rays. A hazy rainbow starts to appear across the clouds, coming into sharper focus before my eyes as the light refracts through the rainwater still hanging there in the air. Nature's mysteries and wild beauty combining to wrap around my soul. And I am lost.

The confusion and uncertainty I felt a few moments ago evaporate in an instant. This is home. My home, and come what may I am not giving it up now. I am staying. I know it. I recognise it even though I have never been here before, and I know it knows me.

My light-bulb moment is broken by deep, booming barking starting up somewhere a way off to my left. A suitable bark to match a dog the size of a sideboard. Leaning out of the window and straining my neck, I try to peer around the side of the house to see what has set Barney off. I can just make out his huge shape bounding uphill through the bracken about half a mile away. He is followed by a small, skinny little girl in a bright red, shiny coat and blue wellies, her waist-length, straight, dark hair loose behind her. She runs to keep up. Every few yards the dog stops, turns to wait, sometimes rushes back at her to bounce at her side, then the two go on together, leaping and striding through the wet bracken.

Opening the window, I shiver in the sudden damp chill from the outside air, and can just hear Rosie's voice carrying across the distance. Laughing, she is calling to Barney to wait for her as she battles on in his slipstream, thigh-deep in the moorland undergrowth, wellies flashing.

I watch them until they disappear over the brow of the nearest hill, then turn and head for the en suite shower. Driven by a sudden rush of energy and exhilaration, I want to be down there with them, running across the moor, soaking up my glorious first morning in this glorious place.

* * * *

Clutching my still-damp clothes from last night's adventures, I make my way back downstairs and through the house towards the kitchen. I need to stick my stuff in the washing machine if possible, and hopefully be able to get it dry enough to wear again soon. Apart from my soggy bundle and my sleeping

T-shirt, the only other clothes I have with me are what I am now wearing—a faded blue denim miniskirt and opaque black tights, topped off with another of my trademark plain black, loose-fitting T-shirts.

Although I did my best with the towel I found in the en suite in my room, my hair is still wet from my shower and streaming wildly down my back in dripping tendrils. I have long since learnt not to go near it with a hairdryer. That just makes the frizz worse. A three-foot, bright orange halo—so not a good look. My black Toms are silent on the hardwood floors as I pad along hopefully, in the direction of Mrs Richardson's kitchen and laundry facilities. I smell coffee, and just possibly a whiff of bacon. And I suddenly realise I am ravenous again.

Standing in the open kitchen doorway, I glance around, expecting to see the trim, efficient figure of my friend and saviour from last night. No such luck. Unless she's tucked away in a cupboard somewhere, the only person in the kitchen is Mr Darke. His chair's angled at the table, one ankle draped over his knee as he idly sips the cup of coffee in his right hand whilst his eyes flick between the stack of papers spread out in front of him and a tablet computer, which he taps occasionally with his left middle finger.

I wait. Perhaps Mrs Richardson is somewhere nearby—maybe she'll appear along the corridor behind me, or come in from outside...

He doesn't move apart from to lift his cup, and once to pick up the ballpoint by his left hand and jot a note on one of the sheets. *So, he's left-handed...*

I turn to creep away, not wanting to disturb his work, and I can hardly ask him about doing my washing.

"Morning, Miss Byrne. You hungry?" His voice stops me in my tracks. "There's bacon in the bottom of the oven if you want some."

Spinning back, I see that he has turned and is watching me intently as I stand there in the doorway, clutching my dirty washing with my stomach growling. I feel like a rabbit caught in headlights, and I have no idea at all why. All he's done is offer me breakfast.

"I... Yes, please. Bacon will be fine, lovely..." I move into the room as he stands, then strolls past me as he heads for the fridge.

"Do you want an egg with that? Bread? Toast?" He has opened the fridge and is looking back at me, one eyebrow raised. "Juice?" He lifts a carton of fresh orange and shakes it, and I nod gratefully when I hear the friendly splashing inside it.

He is casually dressed this morning, but still absolutely gorgeous in black denim jeans and a grey polo shirt, and he is barefoot. He has nice feet, clean, the toes even and straight and toenails neatly clipped short. In contrast, his hair is messy, finger-combed, his just-out-of-bed look seeming inappropriately intimate as we face each other across the kitchen table.

"I was looking for Mrs Richardson..." I begin. "I have some washing and I wondered if —"

"Grace is out. She had some stuff to do in Keighley and took advantage of me being here to look after Rosie while she's gone. She'll be back by teatime, maybe earlier. Washing machine's there." He angles his head towards a cupboard door next to the sink.

Crouching, I open the cupboard to find a washing machine discreetly hidden behind it, so I open the door quickly and ram my gear in. "Is there any washing powder?"

"Search me — not my department. Have a rummage in the cupboard under the sink. Grace keeps most things there."

As there is obviously no further help forthcoming, I root around under the sink and find a plastic container of non-bio liquid. Pouring a capful into the dispenser, I stare blankly at the machine, wondering how to turn it on. A few twists of the dial and random presses of buttons and suddenly it whirs into action. Victorious, I stand and turn back to face Mr Darke, who is still stationed by the open fridge.

"Egg? To go with the bacon?"

"Yes, thank you."

"Fried or scrambled? I do fried best..."

"Fried is fine. I can do it, though — I don't want to put you to any trouble."

"No trouble. You sit down, drink your juice. Do you always wander around with your hair dripping everywhere?"

Caught off guard by the sudden change of topic, I pat my wet, tangled mane nervously. "I'm sorry. I forgot to bring a hairdryer." *Liar, you don't even own a hairdryer and you certainly never waste time messing with your hair.* Feeling self-conscious and scruffy — again — I feel the need to explain, reassure him that I am not always such a mess. "I usually just tie it back. I probably should get it cut, though."

After lighting the gas under a frying pan already on the hob, he deftly breaks an egg into it, then uses a spatula to flick the oil over the egg as he tilts the pan from side to side. "Hard or runny?"

"Oh, I prefer it hard, please."

"Good choice," he murmurs, glancing back at me, and I suspect he's not thinking of fried eggs at all now.

Butterflies explode into life somewhere down below my stomach and I feel a new, strange sensation, something clenching and releasing. Something wet. My nipples start to harden, and I know he notices. He studies my breasts under my T-shirt with a light smile just curling the corner of his mouth, as though he knows exactly what effect his presence and sensual innuendo are having on me.

I curse myself for not wearing a bra—again. I don't usually need to, as my breasts are so tiny that no one can tell anyway, and I am just more comfortable without. But he can tell. He misses nothing as I sit there, inexplicably and very obviously aroused. I grab my glass of juice, using the movement as a reason to turn away from him.

Moments later he is back in front of me, placing a plate with a fried egg—yolk hard, of course—and three rashers of bacon on the table. He places a knife and fork beside the plate. Picking up his cup, he strolls over to the percolator on the worktop to refill it. "Do you want coffee?" he calls over his shoulder, just as the first mouthful of bacon goes in.

Struggling to answer with my mouth full—all I need now is a massive asthmatic choking fit and he really will be convinced I am a total muppet—I mumble an affirmative.

"How do you like it?"

Are we still on coffee? I'm not sure with this man.

After swallowing the bacon, I manage a more coherent response. "Fairly weak, please. White, with no sugar."

He comes back with two cups and sits opposite me, then pushes one cup across the table. And he resumes his work. Totally ignoring me, he turns his attention to his papers, makes notes in the margin, glances occasionally at his iPad and sips his coffee—strong and black, I notice. Grateful not to be the object of his scrutiny for a while, I concentrate on eating, and within minutes my plate is clear.

"Do you want anything else?" His polite enquiry as soon as I have finished suggests he was not ignoring me after all, just not looking at me.

"No, I'm fine, thanks."

"More coffee?" He stands and heads back over to the worktop.

"No, no. Really, I'm fine."

I hear a drawer slide open, then close again, and suddenly he is behind me. I yelp, startled to feel his hands on my hair, sliding over and through its length.

"What are you doing?" I start to rise, trying instinctively to pull away at the same time as I realise he has a towel in his hands and is gently squeezing my wet ringlets, soaking the moisture into the rough, fluffy fabric.

He ignores my struggles, and with one hand on my shoulder he gently shoves me back onto the chair. "Can't have you catching your death," he murmurs, "we have other plans for you. Hold still."

I realise I must have started to wriggle under his hands, overwhelmed by the intimacy of being touched. No one ever touches me, not even my mother.

I can't bear being touched. It makes me feel...vulnerable, not in control. I don't know how to handle it, how to react. All my life I have had to struggle with this, my debilitating awkwardness around other people and social situations, which is part of my 'condition'. Being me, I have read all about this little aversion of mine and I know it is common enough, but that doesn't make it any easier to live with. Over the years I have become adept at avoiding just this sort of situation—never getting too close, stepping aside. But Mr Darke caught me by surprise and has me trapped.

With no way of escaping short of making an unholy scene—the sort of scene that will definitely get me sacked—I have to find a way to get through it. Endure it. Every nerve ending goes onto red alert. I sit stiffly, panic barely suppressed, ready to leap to my feet and run the first chance I get.

Either he doesn't notice my shocked reaction or he pretends not to, since he continues to stroke my hair, rubbing my scalp gently but firmly through the towel. For the next few moments neither of us speaks, and as the seconds tick by I become used to the feel of his hands on me. Gradually I calm down, starting to relax slightly as my brain manages to get the upper hand in my internal struggle and I tell myself I'm safe. I actually start to believe it might be true as he continues to massage my head and scalp with gentle fingers.

Even more amazingly, I realise I might even like this feeling. Sort of. It's completely alien to me, and I know the slightest thing could shatter my newfound composure, but the fact is that I'm here, for the first time in my life, being touched and not jerking away. No longer wanting to. My nipples are once more standing at attention and wetness is gathering between my legs. *Christ Almighty!*

"Do you always touch your employees like this," I manage to whisper, at last finding my voice and sufficient wits to form a coherent sentence.

"Only the ones who are very wet..." he murmurs in response, and I know he is at it again—making suggestive comments to rattle me.

It works faultlessly—he is so good at this, and how could he tell that his gentle fingers are having such an effect on me? As well as the warm moisture dampening my underwear, I can feel heat rising up my neck and my face as his meaning sinks in. I know I am bright red and completely tongue-tied, and I am glad I don't have to look at him or make further conversation. So I sit still, concentrate on breathing in and out and let the massage unwind me, feeling the tension slip away.

The contented silence between us lengthens until suddenly the door flies open and Rosie bursts through it, followed by her big, furry black and brown shadow. And two more, smaller black and white ones. Border collies, as far as I can tell. The kitchen is full of dogs and a laughing child.

They are not alone. A tall, blond man follows them all in, his Doc Martens heavy on the stone flags under his feet. About the same height as Nathan Darke but broader in the shoulders, he is good-looking in an outdoorsy sort of way. As well as his industrial-standard boots, he is dressed in work jeans and a waxed Barbour jacket, open to reveal a purple and green checked shirt underneath. After tossing a bunch of car keys on the table, and placing a carton of half a dozen eggs down rather more carefully, he stands in the middle of the kitchen looking at the pair of us with obvious amusement—me sitting at the table, Mr Darke behind me, his hands in my hair.

"Daddy, I found Tom. He's got eggs, and he wants you. Hello, Miss Byrne. You're up. I'll get my violin after I feed Tracy and Beaker."

Presumably thinking no further comment necessary, the little whirlwind shoots out of the room, Barney and the two border collies on her heels, leaving the three of us to get acquainted.

"Hi there, city boy." I detect a slight Scottish burr as our visitor smiles, making himself at home, strolling over to the table and reaching for Nathan's iPad. "How do you manage to get online right out here? It's all I can do to pick up emails. And what brings you home mid-week, anyway?" Without waiting for an answer, he turns to me, holding out his hand, his smile broad and welcoming. "I'm Tom. I farm across the valley. I guess you must be the violin teacher Rosie's so excited about."

"Er, yes. Pleased to meet you...Tom." I struggle to my feet, take the outstretched hand and shake it, not yet thinking straight and still quivering from Nathan's fingers in my hair.

"Eva Byrne, meet Thomas Shore." Nathan steps in to make the introductions, still holding the towel and smiling slightly into my face as his eyes meet mine, knowing, aware of the moment we just shared. "Tom runs Greystones Farm, about two miles across the tarn from here. And yes, Eva is going to tutor Rosie in the violin over the summer."

"Nice to meet you, Eva. We need a pretty face around here to make up for Nathan's scowling mug." Tom gestures towards Mr Darke with his head, all the while continuing to smile broadly at me—a smile that's genuine, open, welcoming.

I smile back at Tom and feel I might be making another friend—an ally, even, who knows how to put the lofty Mr Darke in his place. That's two friends in two days, three if you count Rosie. And a dog. A world record for me. I'm getting good at this.

"Thank you, Worzel Gummidge." Mr Darke wrinkles his nose. "Are you tramping mud in? Or worse — what's that smell?"

Startled by his rudeness, though I can't think why since he said much worse to me last night, I look from one to the other, wondering what to say. I needn't have worried — clearly this sort of banter is how they deal with each other and both are grinning.

"Fuck off, a bit of dirt never hurt anyone. Is that my bacon I can smell?" Without further ceremony, Tom starts over to the cooker, then opens it to find a couple of rashers still in there. He picks both rashers up, juggling them from hand to hand to cool them, then starts nibbling. "Ah, yes, excellent. I do grow a mean pig. Any coffee going, city boy?"

He looks expectantly at Nathan, who mutters something about "ill-mannered, greedy bloody neighbours" as he rummages in a cupboard for another cup. He places the coffee on the table along with a sugar bowl and a spoon. He obviously knows how Tom takes it.

"You found some fertilised eggs, then?" Mr Darke nods at the egg box.

"Yup." Tom nods over his coffee cup. "Should be. If our Mortimer has had any say in it, anyway. I'll help Rosie slip them under her chicken before I go."

Eggs? Chicken? Mortimer?

My bemused expression must be a picture, because Mr Darke is apparently moved to explain himself. "Rosie keeps a couple of pet chickens round the back — Tracy and Beaker. Useful for eggs, and she likes to keep pets. One of them — Beaker?" — he shrugs — "has got broody and spent the last month sitting on a clutch of eggs. But there's no cockerel here, so no way they are ever going to hatch. Rosie got upset, worried her hen was going to die of a broken heart or something, so for a quiet life I asked Tom if he had any eggs that might be fertile that we could swap for the duds."

I'm astonished. "Will that work?" I ask. "I mean, won't the hen…er, won't *Beaker* notice?"

"Should be fine," says Tom. "Chickens aren't the brightest things on two legs. If one or two of these hatch out she'll be happy enough, and no questions asked."

Apparently deciding that explanations and pleasantries are at an end, Mr Darke interrupts my flow of questioning on the intricacies of poultry husbandry. "Thanks for the eggs. Rosie will be delighted. Now, we're busy, so are you staying long?"

I just gape at him, cringing at his bluntness. My mother would be horrified. Tom is unimpressed, however, sitting easily at the table with his coffee in one hand and bacon in the other, and a wide smile across his face. Clearly he has more to say and is going nowhere just yet.

"So, city slicker—I saw Jack Barlow earlier this morning towing your Porsche down the lane. Looked a bit bent. What's the story on that then?"

"Don't ask." He glowers at me, and I cringe. I had hoped that was all behind us now, but apparently he still harbours a grudge.

"I *am* asking." Tom is persistent, worse luck.

"Fucking hell, you yokels miss nothing, do you?" Striding to the sink to throw the dregs of his coffee away, Mr Darke flings the explanation back over his shoulder. "I pranged it last night, in the rain. I called Jack first thing to get up here with his tow-truck."

"That's not like you, bending your precious car. Anyone hurt?"

"Not yet." His voice is soft, not quite menacing but getting on that way. He turns and leans back against the sink, watching me intently, and I feel that butterfly thing start up again, the clenching deep down. And the wetness between my legs is back. I lean forward so that neither of these overly perceptive men can stare at my breasts as my nipples swell and harden. Christ, this is getting awkward.

"Ah, I see." Tom obviously recognises the signs and can apparently make sense of what is going on here.

I wish I could.

It seems he's satisfied that he's got me, my employer and the bent car sorted in his head, so Tom moves on. "Well, I found Rosie and that bloody mutt of yours on my top meadow. Rosie said you were here, that you turned up late last night, and Eva, of course" — a nod in my direction — "so I offered them a lift back. I thought I'd pop over for a chat, drop off those eggs while they're still fresh enough to do the job, say hello to Eva. And I need to borrow your field again. And your quad bike."

"For the festival?"

"Yup, second weekend in September, next year. Same deal as before, okay?"

"Fine. Email the details over to me, if you can get any sense out of that old steam-driven contraption you call a PC. And what's up with *your* quad?" Coming back to the table, Mr Darke picks up my empty cup and Tom's — which I notice is still half full — then takes them over to the sink and drops them in.

"Busted clutch. Jack's working on it but I need yours for a few days. Okay?"

"Yeah, no problem." Mr Darke wanders over to the kitchen unit and opens a drawer, then pulls out a set of keys that he tosses to Tom. "You know where to find it. And you'll find Rosie, and the hen-run, out the back. Can you see yourself out? I need to show Eva round before I go."

He turns to me, holding out his hand. "Time for your grand tour, Eva. Shall we begin?"

* * * *

"What was all that about a festival?" Tom long gone, the three of us—four, if you count Barney—are strolling across the meadow below the house, towards a stream at the bottom where Rosie insists a troll lives under the bridge. The stream is fast-flowing and full, swollen by all the water running off the surrounding hills and I suspect any trolls have long since been washed away. Rosie seems happy enough when we reach it, though, splashing around in her wellies, assisted by a very wet Barney.

"Every couple of years, Tom holds a music festival on his land. It's a big draw, attracts thousands of people over the course of the weekend. But the council health and safety folk insist on there being at least three exit routes to manage the traffic, so he needs to send some of the vehicles across my land."

"Oh, that's kind of you. To help him out, I mean... And you lent him your quad bike, as well."

"Not kind—good business. Tom's a business partner. I have shares in Greystones so it's in my interest to help him, make this venture profitable. But you're right, Tom's my best friend as well. Even if he is the village idiot most of the time."

Calling to Rosie and Barney, he turns back towards the house, booted feet swishing through the long, still-wet meadow grass. From this distance I can see that

Black Combe is more than just the converted farmhouse I had first thought it was when we arrived last night. It looks to have originally been a substantial house, one or two cottages and a large barn, now all integrated into one huge conversion. There are six bedrooms, at least two bathrooms as well as whatever en suite facilities there might be, the huge kitchen I'm already very familiar with plus three other rooms downstairs. Mr Darke has an impressive home office housed in a corner room on the ground floor, with two walls made entirely of glass. He obviously likes to be able to see out.

I have learnt on my 'grand tour' that the house stands in thirty acres of farmland, and the property includes several outbuildings. Most of the other buildings are still derelict, as Black Combe itself was until Mr Darke bought the place four years ago. He undertook the repairs and conversion to create this beautiful home for himself and his family. An architect himself, Mr Darke designed the house and supervised the conversion personally to make sure he got exactly what he wanted. I suspect he usually does.

One smaller barn, possibly a stable block in a previous life, has been refurbished for use as a garage, and is home to a Land Rover Discovery, an Audi A3 and a fire engine red MG Midget. An empty space is obviously the usual berth for the Porsche, now conspicuously missing. And I saw no sign of Miranda when he showed me the garage earlier.

As we stroll back across the gravel towards the back door we can hear the sound of an approaching car, and moments later Mrs Richardson's stylish little Renault Clio comes into view. After pulling to a stop by the kitchen door, she hops out and pops the boot lid, then starts to unload bags of shopping. Obviously she's taken the opportunity to pay a visit to Sainsbury's and looks to have bought enough to withstand a siege.

After waving her inside to put the kettle on, Mr Darke grabs a couple of bags in each hand and starts towards the kitchen door. I decide to help out as well, and follow the pair of them inside, a bag of shopping dangling from each of my hands. I dump mine next to Mr Darke's on the kitchen table as he heads back outside for the rest. I turn to follow him, but by the time I reach the door he's already coming back in.

"That's the lot," he announces as these last bags join the others on the table. "I need to get back to Leeds," he continues. "I've got meetings this afternoon. Wasn't really intending to come home last night — sort of spur of the moment thing. Still" — his inscrutable gaze fixes on me — "it gave us time to get acquainted. So I'll be getting off soon. I'll take the Audi."

Turning to me, he holds out his hand. "It's been interesting, Miss Byrne. I'll leave you in Mrs Richardson's safe hands. You can get better acquainted with Rosie and her violin. And stay out of the rain. Don't want you getting your hair wet again." Leaning in so that his words are murmured directly into my ear, he continues, for me alone, "Or anywhere else."

He strolls out of the kitchen, then reappears a few minutes later dressed for work. The casual jeans and sports shirt are gone, replaced by a smart, black and grey pinstriped suit, pale grey shirt, dark grey tie and highly polished leather shoes. His hair, which had been loose and waving attractively around his neck, is now pulled back into the severe ponytail I saw last night when he leapt out of his battered Porsche. With a glance and a nod in my direction, he heads for the back door. His hand on the doorknob, he stops, then turns, comes back to stand beside my chair. I look up at him, puzzled.

He smiles and reaches down to tuck a stray tendril of hair behind my ear. I jump, flinching involuntarily under his hand.

"Relax, enjoy yourself. I look forward to hearing all about your progress at the weekend." Ignoring my obvious nervousness, he places his left forefinger between my eyebrows and gently smoothes the skin there. "You frown too much, Miss Byrne," he murmurs. "That's a bad habit of yours. We'll have to work on it. Till Friday, then."

And he's gone.

Chapter Four

On my second morning at Black Combe, I'm astonished when a delivery courier arrives at the front door, asking for Miss Byrne. He thrusts a brown cardboard box into my hands before leaping back into his bright red van.

Puzzled, I carry the box through to the kitchen to find scissors. Three fascinated pairs of eyes watch me attacking the thick parcel tape. And I'm even more amazed, when I get it open, to find a beautiful Rohan hiking jacket nestled inside, fully waterproof, breathable, top of the range. Under the jacket is a pair of ladies' hiking boots, also Rohan, also superb quality. Both are in a fetching combination of purple and lavender. I absolutely love them.

There's a note.

It would be such a pity to lose our violin teacher to exposure. Enjoy. ND

"Oh, how kind! But they must have cost a fortune. I'll have to pay him for these." I blurt the words out without thinking.

Mrs Richardson shakes her head. "No need, love. They're a present. Mr Darke asked me to check in your room to find the right shoe size. Just say thanks when you see him."

I gaze at her, at Rosie. A present? For me? And such a thoughtful gift. So perfect. No one has ever given me anything so beautiful before. I hug the jacket to me as I rush upstairs to admire myself in my wardrobe mirror.

* * * *

The couple of days since Mr Darke left have flown by. Rosie and I have settled into an easy routine of walking the moors with Barney in the mornings, and violin practice in the afternoons, also with Barney in attendance. Mrs Richardson has made it her mission to 'fatten me up' so I am eating like a horse — healthy and wholesome stuff for once, instead of my more customary junk food. And I absolutely love it.

My mother has hardly been off the phone, desperately concerned at my sudden flight for pastures new and threatening to come and check that I'm okay. Quite what she expects to find, or what she would do about it anyway, is beyond me. I've pleaded with her not to follow me, just to trust me and let me be. So far she has. I am thinking very seriously about getting a new mobile — no budgie trilling ringtone and a new number — but that would be just too mean. She cares, and that's sort of nice, really.

Rosie is quite a talented little violin player, and a joy to work with. She is eager, enthusiastic, keen to learn and loves to practise. She is determined to learn to play 'Boléro' so she can perform it for her father like I did — well, maybe not quite like I did — so I have broken the piece down into manageable chunks for her to work on a bit at a time.

Despite her practical abilities and natural aptitude, she has never been taught to read music, so I am working on that with her too. On Thursday evening we borrowed Mr Darke's iPad to download some musical scores of popular pieces, stuff that Rosie knows. 'Jar of Hearts' is a particular favourite, of hers and mine, and she is starting to be able to follow it, seeing how the notes on the sheet work to instruct the player on how to produce the melody that the composer intended. We have also had a go at composing some little practice exercises ourselves, bringing in the techniques Rosie already knows and adding one or two new skills to build up her repertoire.

By Friday suppertime we are feeling rather pleased with ourselves as we sit around the kitchen table, helping ourselves to Mrs Richardson's chunky turkey and stuffing sandwiches.

The crackle of tyres on gravel followed by the slam of a car door has all our heads turning to the kitchen door. It opens, and *he* is back.

"*Daddy!*"

With a shriek and a deep woof respectively, child and dog launch themselves at Mr Darke the instant he comes through the door, and he catches Rosie, swinging her up for a kiss as Barney jumps around his legs. Mrs Richardson bustles around to find him a cup for his coffee — he never drinks tea, as far as I can see — and starts to conjure up a few extra sandwiches. I just stare at him, realising suddenly how much I've missed him whilst he wasn't here. As he puts a beaming Rosie back on her feet, he glances at me. "Still here, Miss Byrne? And still frowning, I see."

Sitting beside me at the table as Mrs Richardson plonks a generous plate of turkey sandwiches in front of him, he looks splendid, as usual—handsome as sin, and super-sophisticated in a sharp, charcoal grey business suit. It's been handmade by the look of it, and I bet he had no change out of five hundred pounds a metre for that cloth. My own black T-shirt and jeans, even more faded than usual owing to them being slung in the washing machine every day, look even sloppier in contrast to his immaculate appearance. I see that his hair is loose now and just brushing the collar of his jacket. I feel the urge to reach out, touch him, but restrain myself.

Gathering my wits and making a conscious effort to appear rather more collected than I feel, I try to answer normally. "Yes, still here. We've been working hard and Rosie has something to show you. When you're ready, obviously..." The poor guy has just got in and not even taken his jacket off yet, and already we're crowding him.

Rosie is not one for waiting, though. Hopping from one foot to the other in excitement, she's at him straight away. "I can play that tune, Daddy, the one Miss Byrne played when she first came. Well, the start of it anyway. I'm doing the rest next week. And I can read the notes on the page. We used your iPad to look them up on the Internet." He glances up at me at the mention of making free with his property, but says nothing...yet. "Can I play it for you? Now? Please, Daddy, please?"

Shrugging off his jacket—which Mrs Richardson immediately grabs, presumably before it slips onto the floor to become a doggy bed—he smiles at her, his chocolate eyes alight with warmth. *God, he really adores that kid. That's so nice...* "Wouldn't miss it, princess, go get your violin. And could you fetch Miss Byrne's as well? You wouldn't mind entertaining us again, would you?" He turns to me, one eyebrow raised.

"Of course not, I'd be delighted." *Anything for you.*

Rosie and I scrape out a passable, but in fairness not remarkable, rendition of 'Boléro'. She is delighted with herself and the proud father declares himself suitably impressed. I perch my glasses on my nose to read the music. *Should I be thinking about contact lenses?* I wonder. *Strange, I never have before.*

We continue to show off with a short practice piece I wrote with Rosie one morning when it was too wet to go out, designed specifically to try out some new techniques and develop her skills.

"What shall we call our tune?" Rosie wonders.

"How about 'Sweet Rosie'?" I suggest, shoving my glasses back into their case before starting to extract my violin from its flouncy chiffon skirt, while she clambers up onto her father's knee.

"'Sweet Rosie'—sounds good. Did you really compose this, Eva?" he asks, peering around Rosie at the untidy, scribbled musical score she has tried valiantly to smooth out after digging it from her back pocket.

I don't want to take all the credit—it was a joint effort, more or less. "Well, we both did. It's not easy finding just the right sort of music to practise and learn. We needed something that had new stuff Rosie hasn't done yet so that she can add new techniques, but also to build on and practise what she does know. So now I've got the hang of where she is with her violin playing, I can help her to write new pieces that are just right for her now." *Oh, no. Do I sound like a crusty old academic – as usual?* "It's important to be able to read the music, to understand the structure of a melody as well as to play by ear." I shut up at last, realising I sound like my old music lecturer and I must be getting boring.

"Amazing, Miss Byrne. You certainly give us our money's worth, don't you?" he says softly, his eyes warm. *Ah, not bored apparently...*

They are all looking at me expectantly, waiting for my next party piece. Mrs Richardson and Barney complete my audience, as before.

Again standing in the middle of the kitchen, I shuffle into a comfortable, grounded stance and position the violin under my chin. Closing my eyes, I take a couple of deep breaths – *in, out, in, out* – and give myself over to the music.

This time I have chosen 'Romanza', a modern piece by Donald Martino, composed specifically as a violin solo. My audience is silent, listening, appreciating, and once more I am in my element, in control, gliding through the haunting melody, sometimes coaxing, sometimes forcing the music out.

I finish and remain standing as the piece fades into the air. After a few moments' silence, they all three stand, clapping.

Mr Darke walks towards me. Stopping right in front of me, he gently takes my violin and bow and places them on the table. "God, you're good, Miss Byrne," he whispers as he lowers his head to kiss my cheek.

Stunned at the intimacy – although perhaps I should be getting used to his possessive ways by now – I freeze in place and forget to shrug him off as he turns and easily puts his arm over my shoulder to face the rest of his household. No one but me seems at all surprised by this familiarity — and it feels strangely good.

Suddenly he changes the mood. "It's not raining for a change. And it's a clear night. Who fancies a moonlight walk down to the tarn?"

* * * *

We have a wonderful time out in the moonlight, all four of us joining hands to walk along the silent, deserted lane, Barney plodding alongside, quiet for once. Rosie's between me and her father, and we swing her into the air, making her shriek with laughter, the sound echoing around the empty moorland landscape.

Mr Darke wouldn't let us take a torch, insisting that the moonlight would be enough to see by. And it is. We let our eyes adjust, open large and wide to let in what light there is, and find we can see pretty well. We see things we would never notice otherwise — the rustling movements of mice and other little night creatures in the hedgerows, the frantic flap of a bat's wings as it circles us before heading back towards the barn-cum-garage. And the night sounds are all around us, quiet and constant, a backdrop to our raucousness as Rosie calls out, "Again, Daddy, Miss Byrne — swing me high again!"

We do, until eventually Mr Darke makes us all stand still and silent, and listen to the night. We tune in to the rustling of leaves, the sound of the rushing beck streaming down the hillside, still full to overflowing, and just once the soft and barely audible whoosh of an owl, which we feel more than hear as he glides close by on silent wings, looking for his supper.

And standing there, in the middle of the lane, our hands joined, we drop our heads back and gaze up into the night sky. Apart from a few wispy streaks of cloud high up, the sky's clear and full of the tiny pinpricks of light that I always find so fascinating. The wonders of particle physics aside, I defy anyone not to start to imagine a greater power and presence at work when confronted by the diamond-studded vastness of infinite space. Still, the scientist in me is difficult to suppress, and soon I find myself explaining and pointing out the sights to Rosie, who is rapt with attention.

"Why are there so many stars?" she breathes, turning in a circle, her little mouth slack with wonder. "And which of those stars is my mummy?"

No scientific answer to that one, and I find myself stammering, startled, desperately casting around for the right response. Mercifully, Nathan steps in.

"I think it's that one up there, sweetheart," he said, pointing at Venus, the brightest light in the sky. "Must be — that's the most beautiful one." *Beautiful?* Clearly he still misses Rosie's mother, and I now assume she's dead rather than simply absent. I find myself wondering what happened to her. She must have died very young. And does he still love her?

Apparently satisfied that she now knows her mummy's whereabouts, Rosie goes back to asking questions about the names of other heavenly bodies, how big they are, how far away. "Are they even bigger than chairs?" she asks, obviously not buying that without some sort of proof. "What about cars? Bet they're not bigger than our house!"

"They are all huge, gigantic," I assure her. "But they aren't all stars." Moving to crouch behind her, my hands on her shoulders, both of us looking up into the sky, I start to explain. "There are quite a few planets up there too." I point out Mars, moving eastwards across the sky towards Saturn, then turn her attention nearer home, to the Moon's craters, clearly visible from where we crouch, gazing up. I point out the Tycho crater in the Southern Lunar Highlands towards the bottom of the Moon.

"Why does it have a name when no one ever goes there?" she asks.

"People have been to the Moon, but not for quite a while," I explain, and unable to stop myself, I rattle on, telling her that Tycho is fairly new, maybe a little over a hundred million years old, and was probably caused by a bit of an asteroid that maybe broke off and smashed into the Moon. "Even though we haven't been there for many years, we know every inch of the Moon's surface, and it is all mapped, every detail. Lots of places on the Moon have names, just like on Earth. There are the Apennine Mountains and the Alpine Valley. And the Sea of Tranquility, though that's more of a flat plain than a sea as it has no water in it…"

I stop, realising—belatedly—that they are all staring at me. Self-conscious, I stand, starting to turn away, apologising. "I'm sorry, I do tend to get a bit carried away. I'm interested in astrophysics, but obviously I forget not everyone's as passionate as I am. Ignore me, I didn't mean to spoil the walk…"

Suddenly desperately embarrassed, I'm gripped by an overwhelming urge to escape, to change the subject, anything. Although it's mild in comparison to the blind panic I felt as I ran from my office in Oxford, my heart rate is spiking and I need to get away. Turning, I start off fast down the lane, almost breaking into a run but I manage to stop myself—that would just be too obvious. I rush off towards the lake, leaving them behind, standing there in the road. I can feel three pairs of bemused eyes burning a hole in my retreating back. Mortified, I try not to cry. And don't succeed.

The pounding of running footsteps behind me, coming up fast, startles me out of my self-pitying reverie an instant before I feel strong hands grab me around my waist from behind, and sweep me off my feet. "Where are you off to, Lucy Skywalker?" He holds me in his arms, spins me around then, standing still, he blows a raspberry into my neck.

To say I'm stunned doesn't even touch the sides! *A raspberry! Christ!* Startled, I clutch his shoulders, scared he might drop me. "What are you—?"

"So, you're a star-gazing nerd as well as a beautiful musician? You take things too seriously, Miss Byrne. You take yourself too seriously. Lighten up—you're among friends here."

"I… But… You're my employer, and I…"

"Well, strictly speaking I'm a client of Little Maestros rather than your employer." I start to protest at his splitting hairs that are already quite narrow enough, but he isn't to be put off. "And I like you. You're staying in my home, with my family. You're pretty, and clever, a brilliant musician as far as I can tell, and a good teacher. And you know all about the Moon as well, so that's a bonus. Rosie likes you. Grace likes you. That makes you my friend, at least. What's not to like?" He lets my feet down and turns me to face him, his hands loosely clasped together behind my back, and looks down at me, waiting.

Well, I suppose he must be looking down at me. I'm staring at my own feet, my head a chaotic tangle of emotions crashing into one another. I'm confused, exhilarated, delighted and terrified, paralysed by my own intense desire for at least some of this to be true — could it be possible that this beautiful, sophisticated, gorgeous man, and his amazing family, might see something in me that is attractive? Likeable? That he — they — could see past the bookish, short-sighted, flat-chested, plain little swot with hair like a bunch of electrified carrots to find something nice? Something interesting? Something to admire?

After a few moments of silence, he tips my chin up with a gentle finger. His eyes on mine are warm, soft and dark. "Are you crying, Miss Byrne?" he asks softly, gently, and I realise I am. With his thumb he wipes away the single tear that has started to roll down my cheek, and bringing his other hand up to my jaw, he frames my face with his hands. "Are you unhappy here?" he whispers.

"No." I mouth my reply, not wanting to break the spell.

"Ah, something else then. May I...?" His face lowers slowly towards mine, and I know he intends to kiss me. He mumbles, "Holy fuck, Eva," before he brushes his lips over my jawline, then settles them on my mouth. Despite the tingle that shudders through me, shooting straight to my toes as his mouth softly explores mine and his breath mingles with my own, the kiss is quick — quite chaste, I suppose you'd say. After all, we do have an audience.

"Daddy and Miss Byrne, sitting in a tree, K-I-S-S-I-N-G!" A delighted Rosie has caught us up and is singing, dancing round us in a circle. "Daddy, is Miss Byrne your girlfriend? If she's your girlfriend, can she still be my teacher? And do I still have to call her Miss Byrne?" *All good questions.*

Mrs Richardson comes bustling up to us, marginally more discreet than Rosie but not even trying to hide her interest in this new shift of events. We all three look to him for answers, for some announcement as to how things now stand. Only Barney seems not to care.

"Not yet. Yes. And yes," he answers firmly, taking my hand. "Now, shall we get on? There's stone skimming to be done at the tarn."

* * * *

The following morning, Saturday, I wake up late. It's the weekend and we did have a late night yesterday. I lie there, my stomach fluttering oddly as I remember every detail of Mr Darke's kiss from last night, out under the stars. And I realise I'm happy — actually, consciously happy for once, as I admire my pretty blue and yellow curtains and the delightful way the sunlight is spearing through a crack, throwing a beam across the room.

Getting dressed, I start to make plans for my day. I have decided not to go back to London for more of my gear. It's too much trouble, and frankly I don't want any of my old stuff anymore. Instead, I have decided on a buying spree. Following last night's highly charged revelations about how others might see me, I am starting to feel just a little bit differently about myself. Nothing spectacular — I'm not about to reinvent myself, whatever that might mean. But I am going to get myself a new — well, updated — image, which will include some grown-up, sophisticated clothes. Maybe even get my hair styled. So I'm going out. And for this, I need Miranda.

Entering the kitchen, I find Mr Darke and Mrs Richardson already there. He's eating an omelette and she has a cup of tea and some toast in front of her.

"Morning, love. What do you fancy for breakfast?" Mrs Richardson is starting to get up, so I wave her back into her seat.

"Just coffee for now. I'll get it," I say, helping myself from the percolator. I feel much more at home here now, and I am used to fending for myself.

Turning to Mr Darke—*I wonder if maybe we might be on first name terms now?*—I decide to grab the bull by the horns, so to speak. "I need my car back, please. Do you know when I can collect it?"

He shrugs. "Jack'll phone when it's ready. If you need a car in the meantime, you can borrow one of mine. The Discovery might suit you."

Not the answer I was hoping for. I want to go shopping. I want my car—I want Miranda. I decide to press the issue. "I'm not really used to driving anything that big. I'd prefer Miranda, really, and I'm sure there wasn't that much damage done. Maybe I can go and see this Jack, find out how long he'll be…"

Putting down his fork, he looks up at me sharply. "That bloody car wasn't roadworthy even before you decided to use it as a roadblock, so don't go getting your hopes up." Does he mean Miranda is a write-off? *Please, no!*

At my stricken look, Mrs Richardson takes pity. Patting my hand, she is quick to reassure me about my precious Miranda's well-being. "Don't worry, dear, Jack can work wonders. We'll soon have your little car back."

A snort from Mr Definitely-Not-on-First-Name-Terms-This-Morning Darke indicates his general contempt for the notion of giving Miranda houseroom again any time soon.

"And if you want, you can borrow my Clio to run about in," continues Mrs Richardson, judiciously ignoring our mutual employer. "So, where are you thinking of going?"

"I need to go shopping. For some more clothes. I can't carry on with just two outfits. And I need..." Glancing at him and hoping he isn't listening too carefully, I continue, "I need some...underwear, and things to sleep in. And I want to get my hair cut."

At that he shoots bolt upright—so much for not listening.

"Where should I go, do you think? Are there nice shops in Bradford? Or Keighley? Do you know of a good hairdresser round here?"

"Ah, lass, you need to go to Leeds for all that sort of thing, or even maybe Manchester," offers Mrs Richardson, shaking her head—I presume in resigned acceptance of the general shortcomings of the more local retail amenities.

Leeds sounds good to me. "Okay, so how far is Leeds from here?"

She glances at Mr Darke, questioning. "At least an hour's drive, probably more. Depends on the traffic. And you'd need to get parked as well. Or you can get there on the train from Keighley."

"Train's probably best. Could I borrow your car to get to the station? Unless you need it today, obviously...?"

"I'll take you." Mr Grumpy Darke is quick to offer. He's finished his omelette and is looking at me intently, his dark chocolate gaze holding mine and effectively shutting out his housekeeper. It's now between him and me, it seems. "To Leeds. I'll drive you there."

"Really, there's no need. I don't want to put you to all that trouble." *An hour or more, alone with him, in a car. And all the way back. I'll be a bag of nerves.*

"No trouble. Not today, though—next week."

At my puzzled look, he reaches up his hand and gently places the fingertips between my eyebrows, the warning look in his eyes telling me in no uncertain terms to be still, not to move, not to pull away from his touch. He gently smoothes my 'frown' away. "There, that's better. Please try not to frown at me every time I talk to you. I've told you before, I don't like it." His tone is quiet, but commanding. Under his words is the unspoken instruction—he means me to obey him.

"I've something to ask you." He stands and strolls over for a coffee refill, then glances back at me, his head tilted in a question as he silently lifts the jug, offering me one too. I shake my head, my nervousness growing at where he might be headed now. "Next Thursday I'm going to an awards do in Leeds. I'm up for a couple of awards for designs my firm did. It's prestigious, a black tie affair. I want you to come with me."

Again, I am speechless. Can he be serious? He wants to take me—*me*—to a posh dinner where he needs to impress business colleagues? What is the barmy sod thinking of? I'll probably throw up on the red carpet or trip up a waiter carrying a tureen of soup. And I can't dance to save my life.

My tongue bursts into life first, marginally before my thinking apparatus, which is usually a lot more on the ball than of late. "You must be joking! Me? At an awards dinner?"

Actually, I have been to black tie affairs before, mainly academic functions, but the principles are the same. Men in penguin suits, women mincing about in glittery black dresses on spiky high heels. Lots of back-patting and false compliments, envious congratulations and insincere praise for the achievements of others and resentment about their undeserved rewards.

And the one overarching reason I know why I can't go to this illustrious event with Mr Darke is that I have nothing suitable to wear. And no idea at all how to put an outfit together. When faced with this sort of challenge in the past, I've usually gone to a dress hire place I know in London and just got suitably kitted out for the occasion. I tell them what I want, what the do is — they usually keep lists of these functions and they know the score. I wear whatever they suggest, right down to shoes and bag. That works. It's an excellent system. They even keep a note of what I've worn to where, to make sure I don't appear twice in the same dress. Perish the thought! In fact, their meticulous record-keeping regarding my formal evening wear history doesn't require a lot of ink.

Anyway, last time I looked out of the window there was no posh frock hire place in sight. Ergo, no awards dinner for me next week.

He clearly has other ideas, however. "No, I'm not joking. I want you to come with me. You'll enjoy it. And I know I will if you come..." *Innuendo again, wet panties again, getting to be a bad habit.*

"I don't have any 'black tie' clothes."

"You're planning to go shopping. Buy what you need. I'll pay."

"I have my own cash, thanks." *I can't let him buy my clothes — that's just too personal.*

I can afford to buy what I need. And I was planning on a few nice tops, pants, maybe a nice skirt or two, not a posh frock and all the trimmings. Shit, I don't even know what trimmings to get. This madness needs scotching. Now.

"Sorry, thanks for asking, really. It's a kind thought, but it's not my sort of thing. I'm sure you'll find someone else." *There, that's me being polite. My mum would be so proud.*

I feel myself starting to panic, afraid he's going to insist and I might have to be rude, let my mum down. I'm no good under pressure, and saying 'no' gracefully has always been quite beyond me. Maybe he's noticed my growing agitation because now he is looking at me intently. Reaching out for my hand, he holds it gently and, stiff with tension, I forget to pull it away.

"I don't want anyone else. I want you." *Does he mean what I think he might mean?* Possibly. His eyes are warm, dark with what looks like arousal. *But what do I know?*

"The shopping's no problem. I have a friend who's a shopping consultant at Harvey Nicks. She'll sort you out. And fix you up with the rest of the stuff you want, as well. And like I said, I'm paying for the outfit because I invited you."

Harvey Nicks? I'm more a Next chick if I'm honest... "I don't think I..."

He turns his chair to face me directly, then, reaching around me for the edge of my seat, he turns my chair too. His face is inches from mine. My growing panic builds. This is so not going well.

"Please don't make a big thing of this," I whisper, staring at my knees where his hand still rests, holding mine. "I just don't want to go. It's not you—I don't like these sorts of functions. I hate dressing up and wearing high heels. I'll show you up..."

Leaning into me, he places his finger under my chin to gently lift my face up, forcing me to make and maintain eye contact with him. I gaze into deep, chocolate-coloured eyes and he is smiling gently, softly. And not letting me shift my gaze away. I am vaguely aware of the click of the outside door closing behind her as Mrs Richardson makes a discreet exit. It really is just between the two of us now.

Still holding my gaze, Mr Darke is at his most persuasive best. I'm convinced he is somehow deliberately ramping up the sex appeal to draw me in, close down my objections.

"Miss Byrne, Eva… I want you to come." He stops, deliberately waiting for the range of meanings of that phrase to sink in, for me to react. Obligingly, I do. Despite my nervousness and confusion, it seems my body is quite certain of its ground, constantly ready to respond. My nipples are already standing at attention.

He glances down in approval, his smile broadening, As if to dispel any remaining doubt as to whether he's noticed my response to him, he drops his hand from my face and he gently trails the backs of his fingers across first my right nipple, then the left. There's nothing subtle in that gesture, definitely not just something conjured up by my overactive imagination. My wishful thinking, even…

"Sweet," he murmurs. "I love it when you do that." Looking back at my face but still stroking the underside of my breast, he returns to the fray. "Come with me."

Yes, okay, I think I might come right here in this chair, in Mrs Richardson's kitchen, if you carry on touching me like that… Please…

"We'll have a good time—a nice meal, a few drinks. I might get a rosette or two and a write up by RIBA for their next review of city living—all good for business. Then we can stay over in Leeds and come back here on Friday."

Stay over in Leeds? Just me and him and my tingling, aching, tiny little breasts that are going to shrivel and disappear altogether if he stops that gentle grazing across my nipples...?

"What about Rosie's lessons?" *Feeble excuse.* Already, I am starting to believe I might be going on this mad scheme, it seems. And I really ought to think about breathing again sometime very soon.

With a wrenching sense of disappointment and loss I feel his hand slide away, back down towards my waist, but I take this opportunity to gulp in a lungful of welcome oxygen. Then his fingers are on my bare stomach as he slips his hand under my T-shirt, starts to slide it back up, towards my breasts. *Oh God! Is he really going to...? I can't let him...*

He is still talking, his voice low, soft as he leans in close to drop the words straight into my ear. "Rosie will be fine. You can give her extra lessons to make up. Or not. I don't mind. Have a day off, Eva. Come with me. Please?"

He has reached my breasts again, bare and braless as usual—*thank God*—and his fingers are lightly feathering across my swollen nipples, first one then the other. He is hardly touching me at all, but I have never felt anything so...*intense* in my life. Gently, he takes my right nipple between his thumb and index finger, rolls and squeezes very lightly, with hardly any pressure at all, but the new sensation is enough to make me arch my back sharply and gasp. As I thrust my breasts forward into his hands, he cups the right one and massages it, first softly, then more firmly as I start to squirm against his hand, moving in for his touch.

I snuggle my face into his shoulder, as much for modesty as anything else. I can't quite believe I am doing this, letting him do this to me. If I wasn't gripping his arms for support, I suspect I would be in a moist puddle at his feet by now.

It seems he knows what I am about, trying to hide from the intensity of the feelings he is creating inside me, and he is having none of it. He cups the back of my head with his free hand, rakes his fingers into my unruly hair, then eases my face away from his body, turning it upward to face him, then holding my gaze again with his sensual, dark eyes.

Slowly, very slowly, he lowers his face to mine and brushes his lips over my mouth, the way he did yesterday evening, but this is so very different. This time, it's just us two—no giggling eight-year-old to interrupt, no Mrs Richardson keeping him in order. *As if she could!*

If I asked him to stop I think he might, possibly, but I'll never know. I can no more stop what is happening between us than I can flap my arms and take to the air. Well beyond sensible thought, I am not sure I can remember my own name right now as I reel under the unfamiliar and irresistible pull of this beautiful man— this man who seems, incredibly, to be interested in me. In my body, my near-to-nonexistent breasts.

I slide my hands up his arms to link them behind his neck as I surrender to this wonderful moment of feeling good and sexy and wanted. After a few seconds he deepens the kiss, running his tongue along the seam between my closed lips, and instinctively I part them for him. His tongue slips inside my mouth, the new and strange sensation at first shocking but quickly beguiling, seductive, sinful. He is delicious as he softly, tentatively explores the insides of my lips, my teeth, then touches and tangles with my tongue as he grows more sure of his welcome.

I protest as he breaks the kiss and drops his hands, but gasp, my eyes widening in a mix of startled surprise and instinctive modesty as he takes hold of the bottom of my T-shirt, quickly pulls it up over my head, then drops it to the floor behind me. I start to cover my breasts with my hands, but he grabs my wrists firmly and pulls my arms down to my sides. He places my hands behind my hips, folding my fingers under his, urging me to grasp the back of my seat.

"Don't let go of the seat, and don't try to cover yourself again, or I'll tie you to that chair." His voice is firm—I think he actually means it. In fact, I know he does. The unexpected surge of wetness between my legs is incredible. Warm, tingling. He lightly tips my chin up with his finger, forcing eye contact again. "Got that, Miss Byrne? Are we clear?"

"Yes," I whisper, almost unable to speak—but he is clearly waiting for an answer, insisting, and I know I have to respond.

"Excellent." He smiles at me, then caresses my naked breasts with his eyes before trailing the index finger of his left hand under each one. My position, with my hands behind my back, pushes my chest forward, inviting him to touch. And he does. Curling his fingers slightly, he runs the back of his hand upwards, following the lower curve of my right breast to the tip, then—still with the backs of his fingers lightly touching me—he gently rolls my nipple between his index and middle finger.

"Your breasts are exquisite," he murmurs. "I love your nipples. Always hard, swollen, so responsive. I've been wanting to touch them, to see them, since that first night. And now I know that they're a gorgeous dark pink. I had wondered…"

Perhaps sensing my embarrassment, he glances up into my face. I am hot, flushed with a mixture of embarrassment, modesty—though that is fast evaporating—and a sense of inadequacy. Never especially proud of my diminutive breasts, despite his kind words, I am not confident that they will stand up to such close scrutiny.

How the hell did I find myself in this position? Naked to the waist, in broad daylight—anyone could walk in! His hands on me, his eyes on me, forbidden to move, to cover myself, and knowing full well I won't until he allows it.

"They're not very big. No one usually notices them…"

His look is gently scornful, as if he thinks I am deluding myself. "Oh, I think they do, Miss Byrne. I did, from the first time you stood dripping in my hallway with your pretty little boobs poking at me through your T-shirt. Your breasts are perfect, Miss Byrne. Sweet, round, they fit in my hands just beautifully"—he stops talking to demonstrate, using both his hands to gently cup my breasts and rolling his thumbs over the swollen, tender tips—"and when you blush—and Miss Byrne, you are always blushing, it seems to me—the glow reaches here too. That's the beauty of fair skin. And no freckles, I see. At least, none I've found yet…" His eyebrow is raised as he glances back at me, for confirmation, perhaps.

I gaze at him, at a loss as to how to answer, or even if I am expected to speak. Probably not, because he leans forward to take my mouth with his again, his tongue slipping straight between my lips to tease the tip of mine, sucking on it until I get the idea and poke the tip of my tongue out for him. He gently takes it between his teeth and draws my tongue inside his mouth — incredible! Suddenly feeling a surge of pure lust, an intense need I never suspected I could dredge up, I want more, much more. I am desperate to throw my arms around his neck and force the pace, but I don't dare move from the position he's put me in.

He breaks the kiss to start nibbling his way down my neck. As if not finding the angle to his liking, he suddenly, effortlessly lifts me from the chair, turns and lays me down with my bare back flat on the table top. He holds both of my wrists in one hand, pinning them to the table above my head and, standing between my legs, leans over to look down at me, stroking his other hand the length of my body from neck to waist.

"Beautiful... Holy fuck, so lovely," he murmurs before he leans down to take my right nipple between his lips.

I squeal, the shock jolting through me even though I had sensed what he was about to do. His body weight and his hand around my wrists hold me in place as he continues his work. The sensation is everywhere, starting at my nipple, which is now painfully engorged. The tingling pulses radiate out through my whole body, connecting as if by some sort of internal electric current to that spot between my legs, which is now drenched. It feels exquisite, acute, intense, forbidden and overwhelming. I arch my back, pushing my breasts towards his mouth, his tongue, his teeth, this source of ecstatic pleasure.

One or two ill-fated fumblings from other students when I was a teenager at university did nothing to prepare me for this. I have never, ever felt anything remotely like this before. I might have read about it, known the theoretical possibility was out there, somewhere. Happening to other women — women who were attractive and had lush, sexy bodies and soft, wavy hair. But this is here, now, happening to me.

I feel the hard table beneath my shoulder blades as I writhe under his skilled lips, his expert tongue and teeth, desperate for more. And he knows what he is about—he knows what I need and he has more for me. Opening his mouth wider, he takes more of my breast in and sucks hard, first one side then the other. He slides his free hand, palm up, between my shoulders and the table to raise me up, giving him easier access with his mouth, his tongue, his teeth. Gently grazing my now helplessly sensitised nipples with his teeth, he suckles me relentlessly, nipping slightly harder, just enough to hurt, maybe—I'm not sure where pain ends and pleasure begins now. What does it matter, anyway? He can do whatever he wants to me as long as he doesn't stop.

He is no longer holding my wrists—he has no need to because I'm lying boneless under him, spread across his kitchen table, pleading wordlessly for...for what? More? Less? The ecstatic pleasure tinged with a hint of pain is so intense now that I can only moan, ride the waves of sensation pulsing from my breasts out through my fingers and toes, each wave bigger, heavier, more compelling than the one before until I am writhing with need.

"I can't. Please, it's too much..." *Is that me? Or someone else whimpering nearby?*

"Yes, you can, you are. Don't fight it, sweetheart, come for me. Now. Come now." His words—insistent, soft and low, seductive—are breathed into my ear before he returns to my breasts, nibbling and sucking mercilessly, building the tension, increasing the sensations coursing through every part of me, winding me tighter and tighter until I burst, screaming out loud as fireworks explode in my head, my groin, everywhere as the earth shifts beneath me. My inner core clenches violently, the wetness surely flooding across the table. I feel I am falling, floating as the tension is released and I hear myself moan in delighted satisfaction, drifting back down towards reality.

Me, the girl who can't bear to be touched. Somehow — God only knows how it happened — I have just spent the last ten minutes spread out half naked on Nathan Darke's kitchen table, his hands and mouth all over me until I totally lost control, and he watched me thrashing about in the throes of my very first orgasm, right in front of him. *Christ!* How wonderful, how intimate. How unlike me. And he's achieved all this without so much as a button of his coming undone.

Raising his head to look into my eyes, which I'm sure must be still glazed from the enormity of what has just happened to me, he smiles tenderly, if that's possible. He drops a light kiss on my lips, then stands and, still holding my gaze, he lifts the hem of my miniskirt to slide his left hand underneath, bracing his right hand flat on the table beside my head as he leans over me, his face inches from mine. He might be intending to kiss me again. *Please.*

Instead, after tugging down my opaque tights and briefs, he slides his fingers between my dripping folds to touch me, gently parting my lips and running his fingertips around the entrance to my vagina. It never occurs to me to protest. I think I might melt.

"Ah, honey, you are so wet, so ready for me," he whispers, his eyes never leaving mine as he slips first one finger, then two inside me. I gasp and tilt my hips forward, parting my thighs instinctively to let him in. I can't believe I'm doing this, that I'm letting him touch me like this.

"I want to fuck you. You know that, don't you?" I can't think of any sensible response to that apart from spreading my legs farther, but he apparently, incredibly, wants to talk! "Don't you?" he repeats, sliding his fingers inside me to stretch and stroke the walls of my vagina. "Answer me, Miss Byrne."

"Yes," I manage to whisper, closing my eyes to savour the intense pleasure he is rekindling, the delicious helplessness as my body responds again, more powerfully still, to this even more intense stimulation.

"Look at me when I'm talking to you, Miss Byrne." His voice is still quiet, but an edge of firmness has crept in too. He slides his wonderful, clever fingers out of my vagina, right out until only the tips are still there, gently circling my entrance, so lightly that I can hardly feel him anymore, before he plunges them back inside me, hard and fast. "Do I have your attention, Miss Byrne?" he asks softly as I jerk under him.

"Yes," I whisper again, opening my eyes obediently. "What are you doing?"

"Am I hurting you?" His tone is low, gentle, the words whispered into my ear.

"No. No, that feels fabulous…"

"Mmmm, I think so too, Miss Byrne. You're so hot and wet and tight, and I want to put my cock inside you, here…" A further deep and fast thrust with his fingers, to make sure I get his point. I do. I definitely do. "Deep and hard and fast, until you scream. I like it that you scream when I make you come. I want to fuck you until you can't stand. With your permission, of course. Is that okay with you, Miss Byrne?"

God, yes, absolutely…

"Miss Byrne?" His insistent voice penetrates my pre-orgasmic haze. "I don't think you're listening to me. I said I want to fuck you, but only if you agree. Will you agree, Miss Byrne?"

"Yes." *Please.*

"Ah, that's good then. I'm going to fuck you hard and fast and deep, and then again, long and slow and easy. I want you under me, on top of me. I want to fuck you up against the wall, and I want to fuck you from behind, bent over a table like this one. I want you in lots of ways, Miss Byrne. There are so many things I want to do to you, and you're going to love it. Well, most of it. I'm going to enjoy fucking you in every which way I want, Miss Byrne. Will that be all right with you?"

"Yes…" Almost oblivious to the crude words and wicked promises he is making, and between his fingers stroking me inside and outside, as he has now started to rub my clitoris with his thumb—*oh, God, could this feel any better?*—I am well beyond coherent thought. Certainly he'll get no argument out of me.

"But not this table, not now…" *Table? Oh, yes, I forgot. I'm stretched out topless on his kitchen table, my legs wide open as he finger-fucks me.* I can't think of anything now except his fingers and the sweet, wonderful things he is doing to me with them—to my vagina, my clitoris. I am going to come again, very soon.

"I want to take my time with you, all the time we need. So not here, not now, not with Mrs Richardson and Rosie hovering outside." *Who? What?* "Come with me to Leeds. Come to the dinner, be wined and dined and spend the night with me. Say yes, Miss Byrne."

"Yes, yes. I'll come. Please, I need…"

"I know you're going to come, very soon. Very hard. And you'll scream for me again. Won't you, sweetheart?" He's moving his fingers faster, sliding them in and out, angled to hit my most sensitive inner spot, circling and stroking my clitoris with his thumb. Despite his instructions, my eyes drift closed as I tune out everything except the feel of his fingers inside me.

"Say you'll come to Leeds with me. Say that too, sweetheart."

"I'll come to Leeds. I'll come." Mindless with desire now and reaching desperately for release, I can only plead with him, beg him to help me. "Please, I need…"

"I know what you need." He bends to kiss my lips again, plunging his tongue into my mouth, in and out, mimicking what he is doing with his fingers between my other lips. That does it. I'm lost.

His mouth on mine swallows my scream, louder this time since the intensity of my second orgasm is so much more than my first was, as I shatter again. My mind and body disintegrate, fragment, the explosion of my climax shooting though every part of my consciousness as the tension he has built and stoked mercilessly bursts and unravels. My vagina clenches hard around his fingers—two, possibly three fingers now inside me—pressing back against my shuddering inner walls to extend my pleasure, increase the intensity of my orgasm. I am at his mercy, totally dependent on him, his skill and expertise, to do this right, to delight me—and he has not let me down.

The sense returns to my body and I drift back into the real world. He straightens, gently sliding his fingers out of me, a slight smile on his lips and his eyes dark with desire. His erection is unmistakeable, large and rock-hard against my leg, my knees still raised, my heels on the table top. I am still wide open and very, very ready. He could most definitely pursue this matter now without any protest from me, but he makes no move to unfasten his jeans. I remember vaguely he said something about waiting, not here, not now, about people outside.

Realising where we are, I'm somewhat belatedly embarrassed again, afraid we might be disturbed. And at the same time I feel deeply grateful, overwhelmed at what has happened, what he has just given me. My first real orgasm. Plural—*orgasms*. And so beautifully done.

"Thank you," I whisper. It seems the only polite thing to say under the circumstances.

"You're very welcome, Miss Byrne" he replies just as politely, bending to retrieve my discarded T-shirt from the floor where he dropped it.

I sit up, perched on the edge of the table, pull my tights and briefs back to full decency, and straighten my skirt. Incredibly, he hardly disarranged them at all, just pulled them down enough to be able to slide his hand inside to work his magic. Rolling my T-shirt up in his hands to the collar, he pulls it down over my head and holds it while I push my arms through the sleeves, as if he's dressing a child. But the impression is one of courtesy, his actions caring and gentle rather than patronising. I like it.

"So, Leeds on Thursday, then?" he states, obviously not inclined to let me off a promise, even if I did make it under duress, of sorts.

"Go on, love. You'll have a lovely time." Mrs Richardson has reappeared. I didn't hear her come back in, so I start at the unexpected voice and jump off her table guiltily. *God, what if I've dirtied it? Did she see anything?* Apparently not, or if she did she's not saying, as she bustles about her ordinary kitchen business, clearing the breakfast plates and empty cups from the table — *how the fuck did we manage not to smash the lot? There must be dire hygiene implications involved in finger-fucking on a kitchen table, right there between the toast and the sugar bowl.*

Mrs Richardson seems oblivious to such issues, however, and goes about her business cheerfully, stacking breakfast dishes in the dishwasher. She discreetly opts not to comment on our mutual employer's awesome erection straining against his jeans before he wisely takes a seat at the table, gesturing to me to do the same. And his housekeeper obviously agrees with Mr Darke that I ought to go to Leeds. He's clearly following my train of thought regarding our unorthodox use of the kitchen table, enjoying my discomfort enormously. He grins smugly, knowingly, as my face erupts in flames.

"Who'll have a lovely time?" Rosie's voice joins the conversation as she ambles in, still in her pyjamas, her hair in tangles from her bed. She heads straight for her father, as always, and starts to clamber up onto his knee. I have to acknowledge a slight — and possibly unworthy — stirring of smug satisfaction at his pained expression, but I admire his quick thinking as he intercepts her. Instead of bringing her to sit on his knee as usual, he lifts her instead and perches her on the edge of the table in front of him, her legs dangling and swinging dangerously. He edges closer to the table, trapping Rosie's legs safely before he visibly relaxes. Oblivious to it all, Rosie leans in to throw her arms around his neck and kiss his cheek. "Is Miss Byrne your girlfriend yet?" she asks, innocently adding to my mortification. "Have you been kissing her again?"

Lord, please open up the floor and swallow me now?

"I've asked Miss Byrne to come to a party in Leeds with me," he replies, snuggling his nose into her tangled hair before blowing his customary raspberry on her neck. "And I'm working on the girlfriend bit. And finally, yes, I have kissed her again. Is all that okay with you, poppet?"

Kissed? And the rest!

"Mmm, that tickles, Daddy. Will there be cake at the party? And jelly?"

"Probably, and music, and speeches."

"Ugh, speeches. Glad I'm not going. Miss Byrne will be a nice girlfriend, and if she's your girlfriend, can I kiss her too? And call her Eva? If you're off to a party with Miss Byrne, can me and Mrs Richardson go to the pictures on Thursday?"

And so it's settled—I'm going to spend the night in Leeds with Mr Darke. And it seems everyone approves.

Chapter Five

We leave Black Combe together a little before ten o'clock on Thursday morning, in Mr Darke's smart Audi A3. *Or should that be Nathan's Audi – surely after the events on the kitchen table we must be on first name terms, at least?*

Neither the Porsche nor Miranda has resurfaced as yet. I make a mental note to nip down to Oakworth, or Haworth, or wherever the legendary Jack plies his trade, and ask him how much longer he thinks he'll need to hang on to my car.

Meanwhile, I'm safely belted into the passenger seat next to Nathan – *yes, on reflection, definitely first name terms* – as we purr away down the lane. My heart is in my mouth. I'm absolutely terrified. And I've never been more excited in my life. My stomach is clenching in anticipation – crushing butterflies?

I felt too nervous to eat anything this morning, much to Mrs Richardson's disgust. "The girl's wasting away. She'll starve to death," she protested at Nathan as he tucked in to his ham and eggs.

He just shrugged, winking at me. "She looks fine to me. Gorgeous, in fact. Is there any ketchup, please?"

"You can't go shopping on an empty stomach, love," she advised me, but to no avail. My guts were in a knot from the moment I woke up and remembered that today is 'the day'. The day I go off to spend the night in Leeds with the gorgeous Nathan Darke, fully intending to give up my virginity to him. And good riddance to it.

There's no way food's going to help. My nerves were already rattled when Nathan drove home yesterday evening, especially to pick me up and take me back with him this morning, although I had offered to make my own way to Leeds by train. Maybe he thought I'd chicken out if left to my own devices. I suspect he might have been right.

So here we are, purring through the dramatic Brontë moorland, all Heathcliff and *Wuthering Heights*, and I am again struck by the sheer, dramatic magic of this glorious place. The day is clear and the views magnificent, heather and bracken glowing bright orange and gold in contrast with the dark grey of the dry stone walls that criss-cross the landscape in every direction, a timeless reminder of the impact of man on nature and the eventual convergence of the two.

"You've an appointment with Damien at eleven," Nathan announces suddenly, breaking into my reverie.

"Damien?" *Have I missed something? Do I know a Damien?*

"Yes, Damien. I thought I mentioned him. Well, maybe not. He's an acquaintance of mine who happens to be a top stylist at Vidal Sassoon in Leeds. He'll do a fine job on your hair, but please, don't get it all cut off."

Completely out of sympathy for my eternally frizzing and uncontrollable hair, I can't help but feel such forbearance would be an opportunity lost. "It'd make life a lot simpler." I reply caustically, but at Nathan's sharp frown I decide I'd better compromise. "Well, maybe he could thin it all out and flatten it a bit, then. I definitely need it styling for tonight."

"He's good. You'll look lovely. Even lovelier than usual." *Flattery will get you everywhere, Mr Darke. Nathan.* "And you're expected at Harvey Nicks around two. The Customer Service Consultant there is called Nicola, and she'll help you. I've already told her about the awards dinner and she knows the sort of thing you might be after for that, but she'll suggest other things for you to try on as well. She has my credit card details and everything will be charged to that."

At my gasp of protest he turns briefly to glance at me. "Don't argue, Miss Byrne. And don't frown." Quietly he mutters, perhaps to himself more than me, "I intend to cure that habit. I said I'd pay because I invited you, so that's how it's going to be."

"But what about the other stuff I want? I can't put all that on your credit card, it wouldn't feel right. I can afford to buy my own clothes. I can support myself, I have done for years." I realise I sound a little on the strident side, but can't help it. He needs telling.

He slants a wry glance across at me. "Not sure I'd call it supporting yourself, exactly, if your deathtrap of a car and extensive wardrobe are any indication," he replies. Then, glancing down at my legs, he adds, "Although I do rather like that skirt, on reflection. We'll keep that."

I flush, remembering how he lifted my denim skirt to slide his hand into my underwear at the weekend, when he treated me to the most fantastic orgasm in my very limited experience.

Not to be distracted—much—I try to make him understand. "I'm not hard up, it's just I'm not that bothered about clothes and cars. And I love Miranda. When will I get her back?"

"Are we back to that again? Bloody junk heap," he mutters, then he's on the attack. "My Porsche's going to cost over a thousand quid to put right. Maybe you might like to contribute to that, as you're not hard up?"

Seeing red, I foolishly enter the fray.

"It was all your bloody fault, hurtling through these narrow lanes in all that rain, in the dark. You might have killed someone—you and your precious gas-guzzling penis substitute of a car. Boys and their bloody toys! Are you crackers, or just a complete moron? You need to go on one of those courses they run for prats like you. Just before you get banned from driving and do us all a favour. And you can pay for your own bloody repairs, and sort Miranda out too. You must have insurance, anyway."

I stop to draw breath. The slight movement alongside me tells me that I have his complete attention. I feel his eyes raking me before he turns back to the road, presumably disillusioned now about his choice of company. Well, that makes two of us.

"And if you think I'm sleeping with you tonight you can think again. I'd rather make love to a toad. You can just turn round and take me back. Or stop and I'll walk back."

"It's three miles."

Smug bastard! "Just stop. I want to get out."

"Probably nearer four, in fact. You've a sassy little mouth, Miss Byrne, when you stop apologising for yourself. I like that. And just to be clear, I have no intention of sleeping with you. We'll both be wide awake. Most of the time. And I never said I wanted to make love to you either."

"Liar! You did say that—you made me agree to come with you today because you wanted sex with me."

Me, he said he wanted me *— God only knows why, but he did say that. The first man to show an interest, and a gorgeous one at that, even if he is an arrogant bastard, and I go and blow it by losing my temper. Shit, the sex would have been so good…*

"I said I wanted to fuck you—hard, fast, deep. Make you scream. I was quite specific. Now do you remember?"

"Yes, of course. That's what I meant…"

"I'm not sure you really understand what I meant, baby. What I want to do with you. To you." His voice is soft now, no longer angry. I suspect maybe he never was. He was just goading me, looking for a reaction. Clearly, I have been outmanoeuvred.

"Then explain." I wait, quiet, nervous, wondering where he is going with this—but in truth, it's starting to fall into place. My practical experience might be nil, but I defy anyone to have read more than me. On any subject.

"I like sex. I like it a lot. But vanilla's not my thing. Not usually. I like my sex with bells on. Sometimes literally." He shoots me a wry glance, as if to see if I am following his drift. I think I probably am, but my gaze is fixed on his profile. I'm still waiting…

"Go on," I whisper, my heart racing.

"The nice, plain, ready-salted variety is okay once in a while, but I like my sex to be exciting, erotic, edgy. And I like to be in control. Always." He pauses for

that to sink in, then does away with any remaining
doubt. Any remaining hope this encounter of ours
might turn out to be the fairy tale ending I promised
myself. "I'm a Dom. A Dominant. I want you to be my
sub. Submissive. Do you know what that means?"

Shit. Some fairy tale... Grimm would be about right.

"I think so. Whips and chains? Gags? Blindfolds?" *I
can't believe I'm actually discussing this.*

"Yes, all of that. Well, maybe not the chains — a bit
too medieval for my taste. And they can leave nasty
bruises, especially on the translucent sort of fair skin
like yours. But the rest, yes. And more..."

"What...more?" My voice is so faint even I can
hardly hear myself. Can he feel my terror? Should I
make a run for it now? Throw myself from a moving
car? *Yes, probably.*

"Like I said, I like my partners, the women I fuck, to
be submissive. Very submissive. Do you know what
that means? Do you know how to submit? Sexually?"

*He has women he fucks. How many women? Christ, what
have I got into?*

The car slows. He pulls into a lay-by and switches
off the engine. In the sudden, deafening silence he
turns in his seat, giving me his undivided attention
now. He is staring at me as I crouch forward in the
passenger seat, twisting my fingers together, trying to
make sense of all this. Ready to leap out and run.

Not quite yet, though. "I think so. Yes. Yes, of course
I know what you mean. And of course I can submit —
if I choose to." There, a hint of defiance. *Go, girl!*

"How flexible of you, Eva. And yes, it's all about
choice, as you say. I won't do anything to you that you
have not consented to, that you haven't chosen to do.
You have my promise on that, so there's no need for
you to curl up into a little ball in case I suddenly

pounce. Relax, Eva. Sit up straight and look at me. You're perfectly safe."

I hadn't realised how tiny, how defensive I'd become. With a conscious effort I unwind my arms from around my knees, sit back, look up and meet his eyes.

He smiles, his eyes twinkling wickedly, as his gaze rakes down my body and back to my face again as I sit there like a rabbit caught in headlamps. "And since we agree about choices being important—and as you might choose to submit, you say—what's your position on nipple clamps? Butt plugs? Well, there's really only one position for butt plugs, in my experience, but, of course, you might know better. And will you let me tie you up? Suspend you from my ceiling while I spank you? Whip you? Cane you?"

I feel the blood drain from my face as I stare at him. I am shocked, horrified even. Did I hear him right? My response is a while coming as I struggle to regain some sort of equilibrium. I am scared, so very scared now.

"You want to do all that, to me? You want to hurt me? But, why...?" With a sinking feeling, something awful occurs to me and I know I have to ask. "Is this still about your car? You're bringing me out here to beat me up because I damaged your car?" I am whispering, I can hear my voice shaking.

At my bewildered, shocked expression, his harsh features soften. His head tilted to one side, he smiles slightly, reaching out to gently stroke my cheek.

"No, nothing like that. Fuck the car."

Ah, right. Thank God it's not that.

"And I won't hurt you. Well, not really, not too much. This is not about beating you up, sweetheart. No punching, no kicking, no nasty bruises or broken bones. God forbid! I will excite you, though. And I will push you to your limits, stretch you so tight that when I release the tension, or when you snap, the pleasure will blow your mind. Pain *will* be a part of it. And so will intense pleasure, so intense you'll beg me to stop. It will never be so much you can't bear it, though, and I'll always take care of you. I'll make sure you're okay."

Close to tears now, I blurt out the questions swirling around my head. "How? How will you know what I can bear? What if I'm gagged? Blindfolded? Tied up? Do you do those things too?" He nods slowly. "How, then? If I can't speak, can't tell you? And what if I ask you to stop and you don't? And how will I enjoy it if you're hurting me so much?" I begin to shake. "I'm not sure I can do this…"

Taking hold of my hand, he raises it to his lips and kisses my palm gently, tenderly. "You're scared, definitely, and shocked too, I think, sweetheart." His voice is soft, low, seductive. "But trust me. Believe me when I say nothing is going to happen unless you agree. I won't force you to do anything. You can keep yourself safe by using a safe word, if you ever need to. It can be any word you choose it but it has to be something you would never normally say. And if you've reached your limit and you need me to stop, you say the safe word and it's over. Straight away. No questions, no excuses. A red light, if you like. And you can have an amber word too. To use when you're struggling, getting near the limit of what you can take and maybe need me to stop for a while, or slow down, ease off…"

I realise it's working. His gentle, soothing words and reassuring touch on my hand are actually working. That peculiar clenching in my groin starts to reassert itself, a feeling that has started to become familiar since I met this strange, arrogant, delicious, exciting, scary man. Despite my fears — and I am dead scared at this moment — I'm already becoming aroused just talking about this stuff. My briefs are starting to feel damp and my ever-present tell-tale nipples are doing their thing. God, what will I be like when we actually start?

And it is in that moment I realise that we will indeed start. I am really, seriously intending to give this mad scheme of his a try.

And, sad cow that I am, I know exactly why.

I'm a thinker, not a doer. A passionless, unfeeling analyst. All my life has been about my brain — my super, overachieving, 'profoundly gifted', IQ of one hundred and eighty-one brain. About what I know, how much I know. And I do know a lot. I've spent my life thinking, learning, studying, understanding, reasoning. Racking up qualifications left, right and centre — more qualifications than I could ever possibly need, but I chase them, collect them because they're there, I can get them, and I really don't know how to do anything else, what else to achieve. All things cerebral, that's me.

But that's all I am. Anything physical, and I'm a wreck. I'm useless at sports, which I can live with. But emotionally I am little more than an embryo, made worse by the fact that intellectually, I completely understand what it is that's missing in me. I understand perfectly well what emotional intelligence is, why most other people I know get on so well together. And I can't manage to make or keep even one friend. Or haven't, until now. I understand all about 'relational capital' and I know I'm totally bankrupt in that department. I know what interpersonal skills the people around me seem to have in spades, and I don't. I can explain perfectly well why everyone except me is able to work together in teams, able to collaborate, cooperate, persuade, negotiate, succeed. I know exactly what it is I'm missing, and that's why it hurts so much.

I might be academically outstanding, welcome in any university I decide to grace with my presence, but I'm as much an object of research as I am a colleague. A curiosity. A freak to be studied and explained, artificially replicated.

My party trick is that I can learn. I can learn more or less anything, effortlessly. And I never forget anything I have learned. That's my claim to fame, that's what makes me interesting to the other academics. And despite all this 'brilliance', my emotional development is more or less equivalent to a goldfish's, as far as I can tell. I'm not a team animal because I don't have a clue about sharing, relying on others, doing my bit. Totally self-obsessed and goal-driven. I can't generate any interest in anyone else's work — only my own.

It's not that I don't care about anyone else's feelings or recognise that their goals are just as legitimate as mine. On a purely intellectual level I understand about being polite. My mother made sure of that, and I do try. I can pretend, for a while, if I concentrate hard and try not to forget to look engaged, but the truth is I'm just not interested. I'll put on a show of listening carefully to what others have to say, but pretty soon I'll lose patience working with anyone who knows less about a subject than I do — and after a few weeks at most of studying a subject I will know more than anyone else around me, definitely. So long-term professional relationships are strained, to say the least. Personal relationships are easier, but only because they're nonexistent.

I have no social graces as far as I can tell. I am often rude, always by accident — which seems worse, in my view, than upsetting people on purpose — and always despite my best efforts to be consciously polite. I'm not liked. Even I don't like me that much. If I'm respected — and it's a big if, frankly — then it's for my weird and wonderful abilities rather than for anything in my personality, anything in myself.

On the plus side, my mother likes me, loves me in spite of everything. In spite of how difficult I am to be around. I suppose because it's in the Mother's Job Description. She's so proud of me, proud of my achievements, and now she just wants me to be happy. Settled. I daresay she wants grandchildren, although she's never said so, but as to that, I'm a lost cause. I'd be downright dangerous as a mother — no defenceless, helpless little child ought to need to depend on me. My mum is always on at me to lighten up, to give people a chance. Not me, no way. I don't let anyone close. I never let anyone except my mum touch me. Except for Nathan, now, apparently, and that's as much a mystery to me as anything I've ever encountered before.

In his house, I have started to make friends. I've found people in this wild place who don't know me or anything about me, but who seem to like me, accept me, joke with me, laugh and play with me. I feel more relaxed, more at home here than I can ever remember. For my whole life, I have felt empty, alone, set apart, numb. I can't even accept my mother's unconditional love without running out on her without a word. But now something has changed. Something incredible seems to be happening to me, around me, and I want to grab it, hold it.

This man is offering me a chance to feel, to really feel something, even if it has to be pain.

I know from my experience on his kitchen table, though, that it will be a lot more than just that. He will pleasure me too. I know he will because I know he can. Without even trying, it seems he can get past all my hang-ups and reach me, touch me. And he is turning out to be very, very good at it.

Whatever happens between us might not last long. In a month or so my contract will be up in any case, and I will have no reason to stay at Black Combe. But, blessed as I am with the power of total recall, I will be able to hold on to this experience forever, and relive it. This experience will last me a lifetime. It will very probably have to. So there's no way I am passing it up.

"Okay, I'll do it."

"You will? That was an unusually easy sell, if you don't mind me saying so. Are you sure?" His sharp gaze is puzzled, quizzical, as though he knows there's more, something I'm not saying. I have no intention of explaining my reasons if I can help it. He already thinks I'm weird enough. And I don't want him backing out now, thinking I'm some sort of head case he can do without, and, worse still, who shouldn't be around his daughter.

"It sounds like it could be fun—well, sort of... And we're both consenting adults. I like to live dangerously."

"Do you?" His intelligent gaze is riveted on me now, disbelieving. He *knows* there's more to this. *Oh God, please don't ask. Just don't ask.* "That's not the impression I've had. You seem like a timid little mouse most of the time, apart from when you're yelling at me about penis substitutes, obviously."

He pauses. For a few moments there is silence between us and I cringe, waiting.

"By the way, you clearly need to become better acquainted with my penis, and I intend to make a start on that very soon."

His blunt sexuality shocks me again, but at the same time I'm flooded with relief to hear the devilment in his voice. I peep up at him. He is smiling. His dark eyes are twinkling in amusement now, rather than drilling through my lies and half-truths, and I recognise sexual appraisal as his gaze sweeps over me again. I smile back, nervous still, but with a growing sense that this is just possibly, somehow, going to be okay. Probably even more than okay.

"Ah, Eva, I am so going to enjoy you," he murmurs, his tone satisfied, relieved even, as he leans in to kiss me. A long, deep, sensuous kiss, full of promise of something much more intense to come. He skims his hands over my upper body, over my clothes — grungy black T-shirt, as usual — then underneath to fondle my bare-as-usual breasts and squeeze my nipples sharply. I gasp, wince at the pain whilst my arousal spikes unexpectedly.

"Shall I take my top off?" I ask. *Please.*

"A generous offer, Miss Byrne" he murmurs into my ear, nuzzling my neck, "and very tempting. But perhaps not, not this time. We're in a public place, in broad daylight. I prefer to watch you unravel in private. And we don't want to get arrested." It doesn't stop him kissing me again, though. With one final, deep sweep of his tongue into my mouth, he breaks the kiss at last and, his hands firm and capable, he carefully restores my clothing to a state of near-enough decency—if we overlook the protruding nipples. "We *will* finish this, Miss Byrne, and very soon," he promises, restarting the engine.

* * * *

Incredibly, we chat companionably throughout the rest of the drive, about nothing much—Nathan pointing out landmarks, me asking questions about the area, about places we pass. We both manage to work around the elephant in the back seat. And the sexual tension is almost unbearable. I am wound so tightly I might just snap here and now. As we get closer to Leeds I try to concentrate on my surroundings, on what's outside the car rather than inside it, between us, inside me.

I am dimly aware of the landscape becoming harder, more built up, densely urban, made up of high-rise buildings, three-lane carriageways, noise and crowds. This is much more the sort of environment I am used to in London, but now it seems quite alien, harsh and stark in comparison to the beautiful, rolling moorland we have left behind. The bleak and beautiful landscape that, even after a couple of weeks, seems to have wrapped itself around me like a warm quilt.

Here in Leeds the buildings are now predominantly made of red brick, the traffic frantic and loud. Everyone and everything seems busy, in a rush to be somewhere, do something. I used to thrive on the excitement of the city, love the buzz of energy and purpose, but now it just sounds like confused babble. I want to go home. To the moors.

Nathan drives us right into the heart of the city centre, somehow negotiating the maze of one-way signs and inner city loop system to end up on double yellow lines at the bottom of one of the busiest shopping streets. Leaning across me, he points to the Vidal Sassoon sign mounted at right angles to a shop about thirty yards up the road. "That's you," he says. "Just go in and ask for Damien. When you're done, get him to point you in the direction of Harvey Nicks. And remember, not too short."

He rakes his fingers through my hair, tangling them in it as he kisses me long and hard. Then, breaking the kiss, he reaches into the inside pocket of his jacket for a business card — tastefully unfussy, of course — which he hands to me.

"When you've finished all your shopping, hop in a taxi and ask the driver to bring you here. This is my office. I'll be waiting for you. No rush, take all the time you want. Enjoy." Leaning even farther across me, he opens the passenger door and I am dismissed, unleashed onto the mean streets of Leeds.

* * * *

Hours later, wearing some of the new clothes I have spent the afternoon choosing, and teetering on a pair of fuck-me red heels — my pride and joy — I scramble out of a Leeds taxi in front of a huge, glass and chrome waterfront construction, apparently the home of Darke Associates, Nathan's company. The doors glide soundlessly apart as I stand there, the gentle waters of Clarence Dock lapping against the dockside behind me, on the edge of what looks to be acres of understated grey carpeting rolling across the huge foyer laid out before me. I enter hesitantly, double-checking the address on the card. Yes, right place. According to this, Nathan's office is on the eighth floor. I look around for the lift.

"Can I help you, madam?" The smooth, polite tones of a doorman flow over me from behind and I turn suddenly, wobbling on my new red heels. I have only a couple of shopping bags with me, and a lovely little black, satchel-style leather handbag I bought on impulse now carefully guarding my bits and pieces — phone, glasses and my seriously underused credit card. Nicola at Harvey Nicks insisted on charging everything to Nathan, and on having everything delivered. Where my purchases went, I have no idea, just that Nathan 'left instructions'.

"I'm looking for Nathan Darke's office, please. He's expecting me."

"Ah, yes. Darke Associates. You need the eighth floor, madam. The lift is over here. Can I help you with your bags?"

"Er, no, thank you, I can manage. I'm fine." I pick up the carriers, hitch my little satchel over my shoulder, and head somewhat precariously for the lift. The doorman, unhampered by fuck-me red heels, gets there first and presses the call button. The doors slide open and I totter in, then press the button with a number eight on it. *Nathan, here I come.*

Apart from the shoes I have a new outfit, right down to my coordinating lacy bra and panties in a fetching shade of red. To match my shoes. These are topped off by a smart black shift dress reaching to mid-calf with a split at the back, and a short, boxy pillar-box red jacket. My old clothes are buried somewhere among the purchases from Harvey Nicks, and I assume have been delivered to wherever, in line with Nathan's instructions.

My finest piece of work today, my absolute triumph, is my hair. My wonderful, beautiful, softly waving, sophisticated hair. Damien was not a good stylist. Not even a great stylist. He was simply outstanding, exceptional. Two down from God in the world of hair and beauty.

Earlier, I slunk into Vidal Sassoon ready to settle for whatever I might get. I've never had a nice haircut in my life, so it never occurred to me there might be any reason to expect to start now. Damien was waiting, expecting me. He sat me down and stood behind me, making eye contact through the mirror and lifting strands of my hair, rubbing it between his fingers, checking the ends. Then he brought a stool around and sat right in front of me, reaching out for chunks of frizz to examine again, pushing it back behind my ears to study the shape of my face, my colouring. He had questions for me. Important matters to be settled.

"This is its natural colour?" *As if anyone would pay good money to have their hair dyed the colour of a Wotsit!*

"And the texture, do you use any products at all?" *Me, products?*

"It's quite thick, maybe a little difficult to style...?" *And the rest...*

Then came his diagnosis.

"It's a lovely colour already, but I could give you more copper to add interest, maybe some blonde and amber highlights to break up the lines. And maybe just a hint of purple..." At my look of astonishment, he actually laughed out loud. "Miss Byrne—or can I call you Eva? You have lovely hair. Long and thick and wavy. Most women would kill for hair like this." At that point I was sure he was taking the piss, but, bless him, he seemed sincere, serious. Deluded, of course, but serious.

"We just need to educate it a bit, so it knows its place. And in return we will pamper, moisturise, shape it, thin it, colour it, take care of it. Trust me, I will make you, and your hair, even more beautiful." I could only stare and nod. *Yes, anything, just make it nice. Make it behave. Submission starts here.*

And he did make it nice. I emerged from the salon some three and a half hours later, a different woman. Gone is the Tango frizz, the harsh shades of marmalade and boiled carrots. Now my hair is soft, the curls loose and gently flowing across my back and shoulders, courtesy of Damien's skill with a hairdryer and straighteners—first thing on my 'to buy' list, a pair of Cloud Nines. The Belisha-beacon orange is now mixed with shades of vibrant copper, honey blonde and yes, even dark aubergine to give a slight purple sheen as the light catches it.

The effect is stunning—I still look like me, but so much more than me. I couldn't help myself, stopping every few yards to admire my reflection in shop windows. Damien has shown me how to twist my hair up into a sophisticated knot for this evening's dressier look, and has even supplied me with a sophisticated, carved wooden claw to hold it in place. But for now I'm floating along, swinging my hair from side to side, my flowing, glossy locks glinting in the artificial light inside the lift. Absolutely wonderful. I can't wait to show Nathan.

Upon reaching the eighth floor, I find myself standing in front of the lift, a carrier bag in each hand, in a quiet, spacious reception area. At the far end, across an expanse of blue and grey speckled carpet, is a reception desk where a rather attractive, youngish man is engaged in what appears to be a difficult conversation on the phone. As I approach, being careful not to get my heels caught in the shag pile, I can hear him trying to assert himself.

"Mr Arzan, please slow down. I can't understand, please... Ayshe isn't here—can we call you back? Mr Arzan, please..." With a grimace, he holds the phone out from his ear and I hear a faint stream of rapid-fire Turkish from the other end. With an apologetic shrug, he smiles at me, then goes back to his efforts to converse with the agitated Turk. It's a one-sided affair, clearly doomed. Mr Arzan isn't going to be put off by talk of calling back or desperate promises to fetch Ayshe, whomever or wherever she might be.

Eventually, I can keep quiet no longer. The young man's face is a picture of misery and frustration, and I decide to offer my help. *See. I can be nice. Must be the Black Combe influence at work.*

"Can I help at all?" I ask politely.

"Excuse me? I'm so sorry to keep you waiting, I'll be with you in just a moment," comes the harried answer from the receptionist—James, it would appear, going by the name plate on his desk.

"No, I mean can I help *you*? Would you like me to translate for you?"

"Translate? Can you...? But it's... Do you understand Turkish?" His look is one of utter incredulity.

"Yes, I do. May I...?" I hold out my hand for the phone, which he hands over dumbly. Watching, waiting.

"*İyi günler,*" I start. "*Adım Eva Byrne. Nazıl sınız?*" Hushed silence for a moment, then without further pleasantries, the torrent is unleashed once more. It seems Mr Arzan is site manager on a construction site in Ankara, and has just taken delivery of a couple of hundred tonnes of substandard RSJ girders destined for a residential development under his supervision. He is not happy, not prepared to continue the build with materials not to the correct specification, and the project is already behind schedule. Apparently Darke Associates are the architects and main project developer, and Mr Arzan wants instructions from on high.

I explain all this to James, who is regarding me with the sort of reverence I suspect he would normally reserve for an appearance of the Archangel Gabriel. Quickly, I explain the problem.

"What would you like me to tell him? James? Do you need him to call back when your normal interpreter—Ayshe?—is here and Nathan has had a chance to decide what to do?"

James just stares, his attention on a point somewhere over my left shoulder. No help there, then.

"No. We can deal with it here and now, Miss Byrne." Nathan's voice behind me takes me by surprise. I spin around, barely keeping my balance on the red heels. He takes my elbow, steadies me as he glances downwards and nods appreciatively. "Excellent choice of footwear, Miss Byrne. And I like the outfit." His eyes rake my figure, which is vaguely impressive in a good light, now that I am aided by an uplift bra to combat the laws of nature.

"And I *love* your hair." He takes a moment to tunnel his fingers through my beautiful soft coppery waves, and leans in to briefly kiss my lips. Is that a thud I hear? James' jaw hitting his desk behind us?

Returning to the urgent matter at hand, Nathan is suddenly all business again.

"Miss Byrne, would you please ask Ahmet to get the haulier back and have the whole shoddy lot shipped back to the supplier? He's right—we're not using subspec materials. Tell him I'll explain to the client. And ask him to phone the supplier every ten minutes until the right RSJs arrive. And to let me know when they do so that I can sack them. Oh, and please thank Ahmet for his diligence — it would have been easier for him to just shrug and get on with it and nine out of ten Turkish site managers in his shoes would have done just that."

"Right." I quickly relay the message to a clearly relieved Mr Arzan, and say my goodbyes. I graciously receive his heartfelt good wishes for me and everyone who is, has ever been and ever will be connected to me, then hand the phone back to the bemused James. Gathering his wits he tries to slip back into receptionist-greeting mode.

"Er, Miss, er — Byrne, was it?" He looks questioningly at his employer. "Who did you…?"

Nathan steps in. "That's okay, Jamie, I'm expecting Miss Byrne. And you can get off now, if you like. After you bring us in some coffee, obviously…" And, taking my elbow again, he steers me back across the carpet towards a set of double doors, and into his office.

The nerve centre of Darke Associates is a huge, airy, minimalist space. The entire outside wall is glass, with views across the Leeds skyline in one direction and the waterfront of Clarence Dock in the other. It's not unlike his office at Black Combe, but with a different view. I am drawn to stand in front of the huge window, gazing out. I definitely prefer the moors, but this view isn't bad. His desk is large, black, the surface polished to a high shine. And clear except for a laptop and desk lamp.

Nathan gestures me over to a conference table at right angles to one wall, with eight matching chairs. James follows us in, carrying a tray of coffee, cups, cream in a small jug and a bowl of sugar lumps. He sets the lot down on the table. "Will you need anything else, Mr Darke?" he asks.

"No, we're fine. See you in the morning," replies Nathan. James nods politely, to Nathan then to me, and leaves the room, closing the door quietly behind him. Nathan smiles at me as he takes off his jacket to hang it over the back of one of the chairs, followed by his blue striped tie, which he shoves into his pocket. Undoing his top shirt button, he sits down and picks up the coffee pot.

"Once more you amaze me, Miss Byrne. A virtuoso violinist and now multilingual, as well. Cream?"

"What? Oh, cream? Yes, thanks." I sit opposite him, waiting for more questions, not sure what else to say, afraid I may have revealed more than I intended to by leaping in back there. But with my newfound enthusiasm for involving myself in other people's affairs, I tell myself I couldn't in good conscience have done nothing to help.

"Get everything you need?" At my look of confusion, he kindly helps me out. "Your shopping? Did you get everything?"

"Yes—oh yes, and the rest. I really do want to pay you back, though, for the extra stuff that was just for me, nothing to do with tonight." *Babbling again, Eva.*

With a shrug, he gets up and strolls across the spacious office to his desk, then opens the top drawer and withdraws a sheet of paper in a clear plastic wallet, and his iPad.

Returning to the table to sit alongside me, he glances sharply at me, cool, efficient. "So, down to business. I want your consent, Miss Byrne. But it has to be informed consent. I always like to make our sort of arrangement really clear," he states matter-of-factly, "just to avoid misunderstandings later."

Arrangement?

"But first, health and safety." *What?*

"We need to sort out contraception, and disease control." At my amazed expression, he goes on to explain, "I trust you do practise safe sex, Miss Byrne?"

Me? I don't practise any sort of sex. And I need some practice. That's the point of all this, why I'm even considering this bizarre 'arrangement'. I just want to get laid. Nicely, of course. Skilfully even, if possible. But laid all the same. And I already know he has the skills I want. So if these are his terms…

"I'm on the pill," I blurt out, realising too late what impression that will create. In fact, I was prescribed the mini pill about three years ago to deal with horrendous heavy periods rather than to prevent unwanted pregnancies. You'd need a sex life for that to be a problem.

"Ah." He looks a little surprised, but quickly rallies. "Well, that simplifies some aspects, I guess. So, just disease control then. I'll use a condom. Is that okay with you?"

"Er, yes, yes, of course. But—I don't have any…"

Idiot. You should have told him you were a virgin. Too late now…and anyway, you don't want to put him off.

Grinning, he leans in and quickly kisses my mouth. "My department, sweetheart, leave the supplies to me." Now, leaning back in his chair again and back to Mr Cool and Efficient, he slides the plastic wallet towards me. "Read this, please."

I take my time retrieving my glasses from my funky little satchel, perching them on my nose before glancing down at the sheet in front of me, at the words printed there. Then I blink, take my glasses off and clean them slowly with the little bit of soft cloth in my glasses case, buying time. He's patient, unhurried, waiting while I collect myself before eventually looking again at the printed sheet, reading carefully to make sure it does indeed say what I think it does.

Words like 'fuck', 'anus', 'faeces', 'fellatio', 'dildo', 'vibrator', 'nipple clamps', 'strangulation' and many, many more leap about in front of my eyes. Snapping my head up, I look back at him in stunned horror.

"What… What is this?" I ask weakly, my self-confident bubble in danger of bursting with a nasty pop.

"Don't look so worried. It's just a way to make sure we both know where we stand," he replies calmly, obviously anticipating my reaction. Reaching out, he takes my hand and turns it palm up, then strokes gently, reassuring me. "Although, in fairness, standing's not generally my favourite position for what I have in mind for you."

His wry humour is strangely calming, and I look back at the sheet full of obscenities, taking a deep breath. If he wants to talk about this…stuff, I can handle it. I hope. I am fully aware we didn't come to Leeds for a picnic by the river, but still…

"We need to agree on the parameters, know what's allowed and what isn't. Do you know what all these words mean?" he asks, still stroking my hand.

"Yes, of course," I reply defensively. Then think better of it. This is no time for false bravado. "Well, I know what these things are. But what do they have to do with me? Or you?" The more frightening ones keep leaping out at me—strangulation, blood, naked flames… "I didn't realise… I mean, I didn't expect… I can't just… This is really dangerous."

"Well, that stuff on that side certainly is. That's why it's on the 'don'ts' list."

"Don'ts?" Relief washes over me. Maybe he's not a psychopath, after all. Not totally.

His voice hardens suddenly. "Pay attention, Miss Byrne, read it carefully. You have three lists in front of you. The first list" — he taps the sheet with his index finger — "here, this explains how our arrangement will work. This is a list of some of the things I want, *intend*" — he looks up sharply, catches my eye to make sure I get it and know he means business — "to do to you. What your role will be, and mine. It's not an exhaustive list, but it's enough to give you a pretty good idea what's going to happen. Read that list, Miss Byrne. Read it out loud, please."

I look down, peering at the words through my glasses, my eyes skimming the list... I start to read out loud.

The arrangement between Nathan Darke and Eva Byrne shall be:
Nathan Darke – Dominant, Top (Control)
Eva Byrne – Submissive, Bottom (Obedience)
General relational context:
Eva Byrne will be naked during the course of any sexual activity, unless otherwise instructed by Nathan Darke.

I look up from the page. "Won't you be naked too, when we make love?" I ask.

"Finish reading, Eva. Ask questions when you've got to the bottom of the first list," comes the curt response. I carry on down the list.

The submissive will obey any instruction and comply immediately with any request by Nathan Darke, without question, argument or comment.
Nathan Darke will take all necessary steps to ensure the safety and well-being of his submissive, including

immediate cessation of any and all activity upon hearing an agreed safe word.

'His submissive'? Not even 'Eva Byrne' anymore…?

The practices to be applied by Nathan Darke to his submissive include but are not restricted to:
Sensory deprivation/control (e.g. use of gagging, blindfold, earplugs)
Intense sensory stimulation
Physical restraint, specifically of hands, wrists, legs, ankles, knees or other parts as required, to include (but not restricted to) binding with rope, straps, handcuffs
Suspension from ceiling or other suitable structure
Punishment and other forms of physical discipline, to include spanking, whipping, caning, biting, punishment fucking
Intercourse on demand, anal and/or vaginal, in any position as required by the Dominant
Penetration – anal and/or vaginal
Use of sex toys and other equipment (examples listed opposite)
Oral sexual stimulation, cunnilingus and fellatio – the submissive to swallow the Dominant's semen as necessary.

I reach the end of the list and realise I am shaking. This seems so cold, so stark, set out in words and print. I continue to stare at the list, unable to raise my eyes. Nathan reaches across the table to cup my chin in his palm, lifting my face to force eye contact. I am frowning, I realise. His hard gaze is steely, determined, unrelenting.

"You asked about me being naked. Any other questions, Miss Byrne?"

"I... Yes. Definitely. It says here you want to suspend me from the ceiling? Like a side of beef? Why?"

"Because then you will be powerless, unable to move. I can touch you, punish you, just as I want, anywhere I want. You just hang there, and take it."

"Oh." *No answer to that, really.*

"The 'you being naked and me dressed' issue is just one of power, dominance, control. I like it that way. I'll probably be undressed when I fuck you, or mostly undressed. You'll get used to it. Your modesty, such as it is, won't last long, I do promise you that." *Such as it is? How rude!*

"And by the time we get to me fucking you, you'll be so desperate for it you'll be well past caring what I'm wearing." *Well, there's a comfort.*

"You said about punishing me. Just now. And it's here on the list—'punishment and physical discipline'." I point to the sheet, at some of the words that scare me the most. "What sorts of things will you punish me for? And how? Will you beat me up if I say something out of line? How much punishment?"

"Things like disobedience, insolence, disrespect. And definitely frowning, Miss Byrne." His fingers are again on my face, smoothing out the furrows between my eyebrows. "This constant frowning of yours is definitely going to have consequences, and now you know what the deal is I am going to start making my point more forcefully. Every frown from now on earns you five strokes, the implement to be of my choosing, Miss Byrne. Does that sound fair?" I gaze at him numbly and, amazingly, I nod my agreement.

Uh-oh.

"What's punishment fucking?"

"That's where I fuck you but don't let you come. You will be intensely aroused, but no orgasm."

"That doesn't sound very nice. Not very gentlemanly. Can you do that? I mean, how will you stop me…?"

"It's not meant to be nice. And when we start our little games, Miss Byrne, you'll soon be quite sure I'm no gentleman. And be under no illusions, Miss Byrne, I will stop you from coming if I decide to. That's what being in control means. And I *am* very good at this stuff."

I believe him. Actually, I'm pleased that he is good at this. One of us needs to be. I don't imagine for a moment that his confidence is misplaced.

I look back at the list, less shocked upon the second and third readings. I think that I could convince myself to be relatively at ease with the activities on the list. Well, perhaps not the discipline and punishment aspects, not entirely, but I know pain is part of the deal. I think I can handle that, although I definitely don't fancy punishment fucking. There is one really big problem I can see, though. I need to convince him not to gag me.

"Is any of this negotiable? I mean, can I just take anything I don't like off this list?"

He leans back, regards me seriously. "What do you have in mind?"

"I'm asthmatic."

"Right…?" He waits, clearly expecting further explanation.

"So I'll struggle with a gag. I won't be able to do it. When I get an asthma attack, I cough and I can't breathe. I tense up, I need to breathe deeply, evenly, control it. A gag would choke me. That's too much to ask. I can't do it. I know I'll panic and start having an attack."

He watches me, considering. "Right, okay. And, gags aside, do these attacks happen without warning? Are there any signs beforehand? Do you feel ill? Can you tell when your asthma is going to kick in?"

"Well, yes. Usually, up to a point... Not always. Cigarette smoke often starts it off. Or if I'm ill, with a cold or something."

"No danger of cigarette smoke here. And I'll make sure you get plenty of orange juice, vitamin C. What about medication? Do you have some sort of inhaler you use to control it?"

"Of course. Ventolin."

"Do you have it with you?"

"Of course. Always." His hand is out, waiting. I rummage through my satchel for the little blue inhaler at the bottom, and place it in his palm.

"Do you have another? Is this a spare one? Could I keep it?" He turns it over in his hand, his eyebrow raised as he waits for my answer.

"I... I suppose so. I have another in my bag. My overnight bag..." After my Ventolin famine back in Oxford, I replenished my supplies while I was staying at my mother's flat—she's always very insistent on that sort of thing—but I last saw that bag in the boot of Nathan's car as we were leaving Black Combe. I have to hope he has it safe somewhere now.

"How do you use it? And what's the dosage?" He is looking at me seriously, clearly paying attention. This seems important to him and I find that somewhat reassuring. I take the inhaler back and press the top sharply to expel a puff of the vapour inside.

"I need to put it in my mouth, this way up, and press the top as I breathe in. Then I hold my breath, if

I can. If I'm coughing I may not manage to. It doesn't matter, I just have another puff."

"How many puffs do you need? To control the attack?"

"It's one a minute until my breathing settles down again. It usually takes three or four minutes."

"Right. A wonder drug, then."

"More a rescue mission, really. And, if possible, sips of water are really helpful. Will I be able to have a drink?"

He looks at me again, reaching for the inhaler. "There'll be water on hand the whole time in any case, Eva. I'll be offering it to you regularly." He smiles at me wryly as he pockets the inhaler. "Subs do tend to become rather dry-mouthed, I've noticed, especially at the beginning. If you need more at any time, just ask me."

"And the gag?"

"There'll be no gag."

I breathe out, the relief overwhelming. Then, "But why do *you* want my inhaler? What will you do with it?"

"If you have an asthma attack while we're...busy, you may not be in a position to help yourself. In that case I'll feel happier having this to hand. Like I said, your health and safety are *my* responsibility. I'll remember what you've told me and I'll take it into account. You've told me what an asthma attack looks like. And now I know about the problem, I'll be able to deal with it."

I gaze at him, wide-eyed. Begin to realise just how serious this could be. For me. He sees, takes my hand, turns it palm up in his.

"I know you're scared, Eva. You're meant to be. That's what gives this stuff its edginess—it's where the thrill comes from, for you and for me. But you'll learn to trust me to look after you. Tell me what you need, I'll do it. It's there, right at the top of the list." He points to the bit about taking necessary steps to look after my health and well-being. "And we won't be doing this stuff if you're ill in any case, with asthma or anything else. It's demanding enough when you're fit and well, especially for the sub." His voice gentles, reassuring. "Don't worry, Eva, you'll be fine. I *will* look after you. Now, any other questions before we go on to look at the list of don'ts?"

Still reeling, I mumble, "No."

He shakes his head sadly. "You forgot one very important thing, Miss Byrne. I'm not convinced you're paying attention."

"I'm sorry, I…" Confused, nervous, intimidated, I look again at the list, searching for any clue that might help me to avert…what? His displeasure? Disappointment? I am already getting a very clear notion of what that could mean.

His voice suddenly gentles and he leans forward, tipping up my chin with his palm. "Safe words, Miss Byrne. You need to know what your safe words are. And so do I. Do you have a word you want to use?" I shake my head, aware my eyes are as big as saucers and my lips are trembling.

"Red, then. That's pretty usual. If you ever need me to stop — whatever's happening, whatever I'm doing, however much I might seem to be in control — you say 'red' and I *will* stop. You have my absolute promise on that. You need to understand that, ultimately, *you* have the control, and that way you can keep yourself safe. And if you say 'yellow' I'll know to take care, that you're struggling. Is all that clear?" I nod, still wide-eyed and trembling.

Dropping his hand he leans back, looking down at me, at the top of my head, now bowed again as I study my knees. "Eva, look at me." I raise my eyes to his, and he smiles at me slightly, his head cocked to one side as he watches every emotion flit across my face. "What are your safe words, Eva?" he asks softly. At my continuing silence he gently prompts me. "Eva? Your safe words?"

"Red," I whisper, "if I want to stop. And yellow to...to...slow down?"

He nods briskly, all business again. "Good, that's clear then. So, any more questions about that first list?"

At my slight headshake, he points again to the sheet of paper—this time the shorter section to the right-hand side of the page.

"Read out the don'ts. I want to be sure you have seen and read all of them." I start to read, slowly. I'm definitely getting the idea of this obedience stuff.

The following practices will NOT be applied or undertaken, in any circumstances:

Strangulation, suffocation, drowning or other impeding of airways

Electrocution

Burning, scalding, use of naked flames

Any activity that involves deliberately breaking the skin

Any activity involving children, animals or other vulnerable/non-consenting individuals

Age regression

Any activity involving faeces or urine (not to be confused with anal penetration).

I reach the end of the list and look up at him in disbelief. It's not a long list, but hell, there's a whole world of sin and pain in there. I can't believe that anyone in their right mind would think any of this stuff was fun.

"Anything you'd like to add, Miss Byrne?"

"Crucifixion? Impaling? Pulling out my teeth?" *Probably not wise to scoff, on reflection. Careful, girl.*

He doesn't seem to mind my brief foray into gallows humour, thank God. "Yes, I get your drift, Miss Byrne. But you need to understand that some Doms are a lot more…sadistic than I tend to be. Some of them really hurt people. It can get dangerous. And some subs expect this stuff. Some actually want it — they like it, get off on it. But it's not for me. I'm not going there and I want that clear up front. I don't want to be carting you off to A & E if something goes wrong, and I don't want to be facing charges for assault and grievous bodily harm. This is a standard list that I put in front of all my new subs, Miss Byrne, so it has to cover all possibilities."

I blurt out the first thing that pops into my head. "Have you had a lot of new subs?" *God, where did that come from?*

"Over the years, yes."

"Do you have any other subs just now?" *I'm not jealous. I'm not. But I need to know. This is important to me.*

"No, Miss Byrne. I dumped the most recent one a couple of weeks ago. The day you arrived at Black Combe, in fact. And since I met you, I've wanted *you* to fill the vacancy."

With an unerring instinct for self-degradation that I daresay will serve me well in the weeks to come, I plough on. "How many? How many other subs before me?"

"Strictly speaking, you're not my sub. Soon, but not yet. But to answer your question — not that it has anything to do with you, with us—I don't know exactly. Dozens. Sometimes more than one at a time."

Christ. No way!

"Will you be...? I mean, will there be others...with us? I don't want that. No, definitely not."

"I'm not too fond of threesomes either, or swapping subs around. And don't worry, I won't pass you on to any other Dom, if that's what you're afraid of."

It had never even occurred to me that he might. *God, what sort of world have I strayed into?*

"Shall we add that to the list of don'ts?" He takes the sheet, sliding it out of the clear wallet to scrawl some notes at the bottom of the don'ts list. "I'll also put punching and kicking and other aggressive violence on there too, as it did come up earlier, back in the car," he adds. "Anything else?"

"Gagging?" I know I'll feel happier if that's clear, enshrined in the documentation.

"Excellent idea, Miss Byrne." He adds it to the list before pushing it back at me. He smiles, then winks at me, his gorgeous chocolate eyes alight with anticipated pleasure. My stomach clenches at the intensity in that look, at what it promises. Maybe. Hopefully. "Now for the fun bit. Read the list in the middle. Out loud."

Breaking his gaze with some reluctance, I look down at the list again and start to read.

The following are examples of sex toys, equipment and apparatus that Nathan Darke may utilise and apply to his submissive for the purposes of stimulation and/or punishment. The submissive will usually be physically restrained during the use of these items.

Acceptance of this list by Eva Byrne implies her consent to such restraint, and to the use of sex toys, equipment and apparatus, at any time and in any circumstances of Nathan Darke's choosing.

I swallow hard, glance up at him. His eyes are intense, unwavering. This is it.

Butt plugs (sizes and shapes to vary)
Ben wa balls
Anal beads
Vibrators (sizes and shapes to vary)
Dildos
Lubricants as required
Nipple clamps and suction devices
Paddles
Canes
Straps
Whips
Spanking crops

Speechless again, whether with shock — surely not, after the conversation we've been having — or embarrassment — more likely, I daresay — I can only stare at the list, starting to visualise the reality of what is to come. Not easy when most of this stuff is quite beyond my experience and not inconsiderable powers of imagination.

With his unerring instinct for knowing what I'm thinking, it seems, he gets straight to the heart of it. "Eva, do you know what these things are? What they look like? What they do?"

"I know what canes and whips look like…"

"Yes, that's the easy part." He reaches for the iPad, forgotten until now, but still on the table in front of us. With a few presses of buttons and screen strokes he has fired it into life and connected to the Internet. Quickly typing into the search box, he navigates to…somewhere. Passing the flat screen to me, he inclines his head.

"Go on, take a look. Just tap on any of the words that interest you and see what's there. Read the instructions, the explanations. Look at the pictures. Take your time." He reaches for the also long-forgotten coffee pot. "More coffee?"

I nod, realising my mouth is dry, and I watch him pouring me a top-up. I straighten my glasses on my nose, then I am distracted, fascinated by the website he has let me loose on. I am looking in the window of an online shop specialising in kinky sex toys and erotica. *Bloody hell! Talk about Dildos 'R' Us! With knobs on.*

"Just look at any sections that interest you. The information about the products is all there, but feel free to ask me any questions if you want. Or not. I'll shut up now, leave you to it." He pushes a fresh cup of coffee at me and stands, then strolls across the office to gaze out of the huge picture windows across the dock outside, before turning and sitting at his desk. I am dimly aware of him firing up his laptop before I tune out everything except the fascinating, forbidden horror of unbridled, uninhibited sexual appetite laid out for my delectation, every whim and preference catered to via the wonders of the web.

I start with vibrators. That seems safe enough, and I do at least know what those are. Correction — I thought I knew. The first one I see is a cool-looking little item, sort of U-shaped, which is apparently designed to slip one end inside my vagina during intercourse, the other end vibrating against my clitoris. *Holy fuck! I wonder if he has one of those. Please.*

There's more. Much more. DIY vibrators in all shapes, sizes and colours, guaranteed to produce amazing orgasms. Vibrating eggs, clitoral vibrators, some designed to be switched on remotely — I need to think that through — finger vibrators, G-spot vibrators...the range seems endless.

Dragging myself away from the breathtaking array of erotic choices, I turn to nipple toys. That should cool me down.

Wrong again. I find vibrating nipple clamps in various shades of pink, purple, blue. Nipple rings, chains, pumps to simulate sucking. *Sweet Jesus and Mary! And Joseph!*

There's a section on anal stimulation. I must confess that concept has been a bit difficult to grasp so far, so I venture in there, among the butt plugs — again all colours of the rainbow, shapes, sizes, some vibrating, naturally — and anal beads. Amazing!

Who needs the likes of Nathan Darke when there are shops like this in the world, selling these wonderful DIY experiences? Why haven't I found all this out before now?

Leaning back in my chair, I realise he has come to stand behind me. He is looking at the screen. How long has he been there? He bends to whisper in my ear. "Anything you particularly fancy?"

Christ, yes!

"Show me." *Oh, did I say that out loud?*

"Eva? What do you like the look of?"

Unabashed, I go back to the vibrators page, to the lovely little U-shaped gizmo. "That. That looks...fun."

"Definitely does. What colour would you like?" At my stunned silence, he leans over me to tap the screen, quickly adding a purple one to his basket. *Bloody hell, it costs fifty-four quid.*

"What else do we need?"

"I...don't know. Don't you have this, this...stuff already?"

"Mmm, I do have lots of this stuff. You're welcome to anything of mine you'd like to try. And I'll certainly bring out a few of my favourites. But it's nice to choose some of your own. So, what else would you like, Eva? Did you check out the whips? The canes?"

"I... Yes."

"Well?"

"What about a feather thing? They looked okay..." Innocuous enough, hopefully.

"Wimp. You'll find I can do some amazing things to you with feathers." He taps the screen as the bondage toys page re-emerges, and he selects a feather tickler and a suede flogger. I shudder as a rattan cane and a spanking crop join our growing collection. "What else did you look at, Eva?"

I go back to the nipple clamps. They look sort of fierce, but fascinating. "Do these hurt?"

"Yes, if they are tight. Most are adjustable, though. But tight's good. Like this." He slips his right hand down the front of my dress to cup my left breast, gently caressing my uplifted curves over my new, gravity-defying bra before nudging it aside and taking my nipple between his fingertips. He rolls it gently, then more firmly, increasing the pressure with his fingers until I wince, sucking in my breath sharply.

"Did I hurt you?"

"Yes, a little." He squeezes again, harder still. I gasp, but don't pull away this time.

"Still hurting?"

"Yes. No."

"Shall I stop?"

"No, please don't stop." My voice is a whisper, my head back against his shoulder, my eyes closed.

"With nipple clamps I wouldn't have to stop. I could leave you gasping, your beautiful, sexy nipples well attended to, while I'm busy elsewhere. On your clit, for example. Or I could spank you while your nipples are clamped. That would be so erotic—just imagine…"

Is that me moaning? I can feel the moisture pooling between my legs at his filthy, erotic imagery, at his fingers still squeezing my nipples hard, mercilessly. *Oh my word!*

"I think we need nipple clamps, don't you? Nice pink ones with vibrating bullets suspended from them. Vibrating bullets are great on your clitoris too. Very versatile," he whispers in my ear.

I can only nod as he clicks on the item and adds it to the basket.

"Now what? Butt plugs? A girl should have her own personal butt plugs, I think. More hygienic. Don't you agree, Miss Byrne?" He never lets up the pressure on my nipple, squeezing it between his fingers whilst his thumb rubs the tip, hard, as he swiftly adds more products to the basket. "And some anal beads, I think. Very interesting sensation. You'll like those. Would you care to bend over the table and lift your skirt, Miss Byrne, let me demonstrate?"

What? Now? "Do you have some handy?" *Did I actually say that?*

"Never leave home without them, Miss Byrne. But maybe now's not the time. Definitely something to look forward to, though. Have we finished shopping?"

I nod, desperately writhing against his hand.

"Okay." He taps the screen a few more times to complete the purchases. Then, slipping his hand out of my bra, he pulls me to my feet and quickly turns me to face the table. His hand in the small of my back, he pushes me face down across the hardwood surface, sliding the iPad and my coffee cup to one side.

I start in surprise as he lifts the hem of my dress — surely he just said...

Then I moan out loud as he again slips his hand into my clothing, this time down the back of my lovely red lacy briefs, down the hollow between my buttocks, slowing slightly to circle my anus with one gentle fingertip. I stiffen, waiting...

"So sweet and tight. We'll come back to this," he murmurs softly, leaning close to kiss my neck before continuing on between the wet, swollen lips of my vagina. He slips one finger inside my moist entrance, working gently in and out, circling the outer lips, spreading my juices all around. I moan faintly, lifting my bum up in welcome. He slides a second finger inside, whilst with his other hand he attacks from the front to take my swollen clitoris between his thumb and finger, gently rubbing.

The combined pleasure is so intense, so centred, so sudden, it overwhelms me and I come immediately. I scream, unable to contain any of the fabulous sensation of internal fragmentation now shooting out through my outstretched fingers — white-knuckled, still gripping the edge of the table — and my toes, still encased in my lovely, red fuck-me shoes. I whimper, almost in frustration that my climax has hit me before I even saw it coming.

"I'm not finished with you yet. Stay there."

More? How wonderful.

His voice is low, seductive and commanding. I stay still. Waiting. He straightens, steps away from me, goes over to his desk. He returns a moment later, gently pulling my underwear down to my ankles. "Step out." His command is clear. I obey.

"You have a beautiful bottom, Miss Byrne," he observes, trailing his fingertips lightly down the furrow between my buttocks, then tracing the line of each lower curve before bringing something down on me—hard, sharp, fierce. I scream out loud, with shock more than pain, though the sting is real enough. Instinctively I start to stand up, but his hand goes to the small of my back, pressing me back down.

"We agreed on five strokes for every frown. I counted at least four frowns since we came into this room, and that's me being generous, Miss Byrne. So that's twenty strokes. Agreed?"

I don't answer, still reeling from the sudden assault. He strikes me again, and I scream again, louder. "Agreed, Miss Byrne?"

"Yes, yes. Please don't…"

"Eighteen to go, then. Grit your teeth, Miss Byrne."

I do, flinching with every blow, my fingers curled desperately around the opposite edge of the table. Counting slowly. He takes his time, waiting between each blow for me to settle again, to be ready. After ten strokes he stops, places a ruler beside my face on the table, and steps away again. I know not to move. He comes back after a few moments and I feel something cool, soothing, being smoothed into my red-hot and extremely sore buttocks. He gently massages me, kneading my tender skin where his ruler has done its work.

"You're new to this, Miss Byrne, so I'm really being very gentle with you. Next time it will be harder." He taps my buttock lightly with his palm. "Relax—we'll soon be done." He stands, picks up the ruler again. "Are you ready to continue, Miss Byrne?"

I know he will demand an answer so I whisper my consent, and he starts again. The next ten blows are excruciating. He alternates between bringing his ruler down hard on first one side of my bottom, then the other, always hitting the same spot on each cheek and now not even waiting for me to collect myself between blows. Each new blow builds on the sting left by the one before it. I lie there in my world of pain, biting my lip to keep from sobbing, waiting for him to finish.

After the twentieth stroke he straightens, stands still behind me. I can imagine his eyes on my abused bottom, and just hope he's satisfied. I know better than to say as much, though, and I wait, desperate for him to give me permission to get up. I lie there, frozen with dread at what might be coming next.

"Open your legs, Eva."

I comply, too scared to resist. Tense, shaking, I can feel the tears streaming from my eyes. Am I about to lose my virginity here, humiliated and hurting, facedown on a table, trying not to sob out loud? *Please, no, not like this…*

"Wider, Eva."

I force myself to spread my legs as far as I can. There's no point arguing. His fingers are on me, gently opening the lips of my vagina. I gulp, tensing, waiting for the pain I know is coming. I feel something slip easily inside me. It's not… What is it?

"Aaah!" My gasp is one of shock, not pain, as I feel vibrations start to pulse through me, from my inner core radiating outwards. He is standing now, not touching me, his hands flat on the table on either side of my head. He leans down to kiss the back of my neck, to whisper in my ear, "Enjoy, Eva. You've earned it."

Gently, firmly, he runs his hands all over my back, massaging, comforting. Reaching lower, he smoothes some more cooling cream into my buttocks. I sigh, writhing with pleasure and need as the internal pulsing gathers strength, massaging my internal walls too. "Oh, yes, please, please…" I am almost mindless with desire as he reaches around me to lightly feather his fingertips across my clitoris. Little by little, any remaining pain dissipates and the sensuous delight builds, growing, reaching farther and wider into my inner self. I am desperate with need, murmuring incoherently, begging him to help me.

"Tell me what you want, Eva. What is it you need?"

"I want… I want you to… Oh, yes, that's so good." The pulsing of the vibrator inside my vagina is so strong now, urgent, unrelenting, irresistible. I know my orgasm isn't far away. My hips are jerking, trying to increase the pressure on my clitoris, but he keeps his touch featherlight, teasing me, tantalising me.

"Please…" I'm desperate, so very desperate…

"Is this what you want?" He increases the pressure, only slightly, but enough to have my clitoris leaping to attention, swollen, seeking.

He circles my greedy clit with his finger, once, twice. Then, merciful at last, he takes it between his fingers and thumb and rolls it firmly. The result is instantaneous. My orgasm goes off like a volcano, my hips thrusting and gyrating for long moments as I ride the waves of intense pleasure flowing freely through me. I might even have lost consciousness towards the end, because the next thing I am aware of is the sensation of the vibrator, silent and still now, as Nathan slides it out of my vagina. Too spent to move, I am still lying draped over the table, boneless and very, very satisfied.

And as my brainpower returns to something like normal — whatever that is these days — I feel overwhelming relief to have come through my first 'test' relatively unscathed.

"Can you stand, Eva?" he asks me, wryly adding, "You certainly won't be able to sit for a while."

Using my hands to lever myself up off the table, I slowly get to my feet. My skirt drops back down over my bottom, and at least outwardly I am decent again. *Good God, what just happened?*

His hands on my shoulders, Nathan turns me to face him. Then, taking my face between his hands, he lifts it carefully, looks into my eyes. "You've been crying, sweetheart," he says, gently wiping my remaining tears with his thumbs before dropping his lips to mine.

Despite all that has just happened, all he has done to me, the pain is forgotten as I melt under his kiss. My arms come up of their own volition and I clasp my hands behind his neck, holding onto him for dear life, because otherwise, I am definitely going to hit the carpet at his feet. I open my mouth under his. His tongue darts inside, stroking me, dancing with mine, tasting me. He sucks my bottom lip into his mouth, playing with me, and I respond as always. Despite everything.

Breaking the kiss, he nuzzles my neck. "Are we okay, sweetheart?" he asks me. "Am I forgiven? Did I make up for it?"

My answer is to turn my head and capture his mouth, initiating my first kiss with him rather than just responding to his. He tightens his arms around me, and this time I let my tongue go exploring. I am deliriously happy.

After long, dragging moments he lifts his head, nudges his nose playfully against mine. His eyes are warm, deep and sensual, drawing me in.

"Welcome to the Dark Side, Miss Byrne."

Chapter Six

We are on the way to the penthouse suite on the fourteenth floor of the same building, six floors up from Nathan's offices. After I managed to stop my tears from streaming and get my legs steady enough under me to make walking a possibility, Nathan picked up my discarded pants, slipped them into his pocket with a knowing smirk—no way could I face pulling them across my still painfully tender backside—and held out his hand to me. I took it and followed him, out through the empty reception area and back into the outer foyer. He called the lift and we stepped in.

I expected us to be going down, heading for some hotel somewhere, so I am surprised when I feel the upwards motion under my feet. Nathan just stands silently beside me, leaning on the mirrored side of the lift.

I catch my reflection beside him, and am startled. Is that me? Really me, that woman with the beautiful, flowing hair, looking smart and willowy in lovely, flattering, sophisticated clothes, four inches taller in my outrageous heels? Is that really me, my face slightly flushed and tear-stained from having just been thoroughly thrashed across my naked bottom, then kissed stupid by this gorgeous man at my side?

Nathan's face is stern, his chin tipped up to watch the numbers changing above the door. I quake a little. Have I done something to get on the wrong side of him again? He's completely mercurial, his rapidly changing moods more than I can keep track of. I only have one mood these days, I reckon—apprehensive. I have had this mood for a while, come to think of it—definitely since leaving St Hilda's, and even more so since arriving at Black Combe. I used to be so sure of things, of where I stood and what I stood for, hollow though that was, as I've now started to realise. And this wonderful, intimidating, stunningly gorgeous, harsh man beside me is confronting and kicking aside every certainty I ever thought I had. Every value I might hold. Every principle about equality, dignity, respect.

God, how absolutely wonderful.

The lift glides to a halt and we step out onto the fourteenth floor, into the penthouse suite on the roof. There's only one door off this landing, and Nathan opens it with a key card. He gestures me to precede him inside, following me in. The door clicks shut behind us, locking automatically.

"Wow, whose apartment is this? This place is so cool!" I stand in the middle of the enormous living area, turning on the spot, taking in the huge picture windows making up all of one wall and offering superb views across the rooftop patio, over Clarence Dock and for about half a mile, to the skyline of Leeds city centre.

At one end of the apartment is a state-of-the-art kitchen with magnificent granite worktops—perfectly free of clutter, obviously—and a large, dinner-party-standard dining area. I note the sturdy-looking oak table with some trepidation, and have no doubt that I will find myself sprawled across that sometime very soon.

The cream-coloured carpet is deep and plush, and I feel I ought to take off my shoes, although Nathan doesn't seem to care. He strolls in behind me, his jacket over his arm, and tosses his key card onto a small table just inside the door.

"It's mine. I used to live here permanently before I moved to Black Combe. I keep the place because it's more comfortable than hotels when I want to stay over in Leeds. And it's handy for the office. I'm usually here a couple of nights a week." He walks around, obviously very much at home, switching on lamps. Moving into the kitchen area, he flicks the switch on the kettle. "Tea? Coffee?" He looks at me expectantly, the perfect host.

"Tea, please. Earl Grey if you have it." I am still gazing around me in bewildered admiration. "This place suits you." I glance at him, catch the raised eyebrow. He's right, of course—how on earth would I know what sort of place suits Mr Nathan Darke? Undaunted, I blunder on—social skills and sensitivity were never my forte. "I can see you living here more than I can picture you at Black Combe. But Black Combe seems like your family home…"

Deftly tipping boiling water into two cups, he replies over his shoulder, "Black Combe *is* my family home, now. I bought it as a derelict ruined farm and did the renovations about four years ago. When I adopted Rosie."

He glances back at me, taking in my stunned silence at his bombshell. *Adopted.*

At my open-mouthed silence, he goes on with his explanation. "City centre living is great for a single bloke living alone. It's ideal if all you want is the nightlife, the bars and theatres and clubs…" He looks over at me again, briefly distracted from his efforts around the teacups and hot water — waiting, no doubt, for me to realise what sort of clubs he probably means. I couldn't be less interested in that just now. *Adopted!*

I find my voice at last and, delicate as ever, blurt out what's on my mind. "Adopted Rosie? You mean you're not her father?"

"Not in the beginning. But I am now," comes his curt response. He returns to his explanation. "And city living's no good at all for a small child. Kids need childcare, schools, doctors, dentists, other kids to play with, safe places to play out. Most city-dwellers move out to the sticks when the kids start arriving. We're a pretty transient community here. I wanted a decent home for Rosie, a place she could grow up happy, healthy, safe, with plenty of space and fresh air. So I decided to keep Black Combe instead of just renovating it and selling it on. Grace — Mrs Richardson — was my housekeeper here at the apartment, and she moved with us."

He comes back across the room with my tea, and hands the steaming cup to me. "Careful, it's hot. Your stuff is in the spare room. I'll show you."

The important revelations obviously finished for now, he holds my gaze while I can only stare. Try to take in what he has said.

Including… *Did he say 'stuff'?*

Picking up on my confusion again, and helpful as ever, not to mention patient, he explains. "Your shopping, the stuff from Harvey Nicks. I got Nicola to have it all delivered here. Charles brought it up and put it in the spare room."

"Charles?" Stupid question, but it pops out anyway.

"The doorman, from downstairs. He took delivery of all your purchases and brought them up to the apartment for me. Here…" Strolling across the apartment, he opens a door off the central living room and I catch a glimpse of a double bed piled high with Harvey Nichols carrier bags. *Did I really buy all that? Christ!* I follow him across the apartment and peer around him into the bedroom.

Switching back to mine genial host again, he gestures me into the spare bedroom, apparently mine for the duration. This is not the arrangement I'd expected, actually. I tell myself I'm relieved rather than disappointed, but even I know better than to believe that.

His grin is knowing as he continues, "We need to go out in about two hours, so you've time for a long soak if you want. Help to take the sting out of your aching bones." He smiles, gently rubbing my backside before planting a friendly kiss on my cheek.

"Enjoy your tea. And your bath. I have some work to finish." And with that, he leaves me to admire my purchases and pander to my 'aching bones'. He closes the door, leaving me to it.

* * * *

One long soak and several cups of delicate Earl Grey later, I am ready. Standing in the middle of the guest room, in front of the full-length mirrored wardrobe door, I slowly turn, admiring. I have scrubbed up well, even if I do say so myself.

Nicola's advice was spot on. She picked out the stunning ankle-length, Grecian-style, emerald green dress now draped over my slender figure. I'm still thin, no avoiding that, but the underwired, strapless bra Nicola teamed with the dress is doing a sterling job and I have curves for once. Real curves. Sexy curves.

The dress is draped over one shoulder, leaving the other shoulder bare, and is gathered in soft folds around my waist before falling softly to trail the floor behind me. The deep V-shaped neckline feels sensuous, risky, and the low back not much short of indecent. My toes peek out of the front, in pretty, gold, strappy sandals. A matching gold link belt hangs loosely around my waist. My hair — the new, brightly highlighted autumn colours set off perfectly by the vivid green shade of my dress — has at last submitted to my ministrations and gone into a loose topknot, a few tendrils framing my face. I have never, ever before won a fight with my hair. Those straighteners got it right — I *am* on Cloud Nine.

Still, the proof of the pudding and all that — I've yet to get the seal of approval from *him*. Nathan has left me alone since we arrived, but I have heard him moving around the apartment, in the shower, pottering in the kitchen. He was nowhere in sight, though, each time I ventured out to replenish my Earl Grey levels.

With a deep breath, my shoulders back and chin high, I open the bedroom door and step out into the living room. He is there, splendid in black evening dress, at the kitchen worktop with his back to me. Hearing the door, he turns.

"Holy shit!" His eyes are wide, appraising, instantly aroused. He stands, his gaze slowly moving from my hair down to my toes and back, lingering at my hips, my breasts. "Turn around," he breathes quietly. I do, standing still to let him see my handiwork—and Nicola's, and Damien's—from every angle. I sense his soft footfalls across the carpet as he approaches, but I force myself not to turn. To wait for his verdict.

"Eva, you are beautiful. Absolutely stunning. You take my breath away." His lips brush the sensitive skin on the back of my neck, the backs of my ears. I shiver.

His hands on my shoulders, he gently turns me, kisses my mouth. His tongue slips in, familiar now, tangling with mine, his hands cupping the back of my head to keep me still as he deepens the kiss. I rest my hands on his forearms, sinking into the sensuality of the moment. He says I'm beautiful, and in that moment I do feel absolutely stunning. And stunned. I want to pinch myself, just to check this really is me in this gorgeous dress, being kissed senseless by this gorgeous man.

Breaking the kiss, he murmurs in my ear, "How's your bum? Still sore?"

"Yes...a little."

"Are you wearing knickers?"

"Yes, of course!"

"Take them off."

"What? You want to...? Now...?" I'm not about to argue, I suppose—but really, I'd have preferred his attentions before I put all that effort into my hair.

He chuckles, reading my thoughts from my expression, as usual. "What, and muss you up? When you've gone to so much trouble? No, but you'll be more comfortable without them. And who's to know except me? And, sweetheart, I love the idea that you'll be naked under that dress. So drop 'em. Please."

I can see his point. And he did ask nicely, so I do as he suggests, leaning on his arm to step out. He picks my discarded panties up, admiring the delicate pink and pale green lace confection before placing them on the worktop.

He cups my face in his hands, his pupils large with desire, just inches from mine. "This is going to be a long evening," he groans, before kissing me again.

* * * *

It isn't, though. It flies past. And I have a wonderful time.

I expected to be hopping into a taxi, or even Nathan's Audi, but instead we walk. The dinner is being held at the Royal Armouries, Leeds' flagship museum housing all things military and weapon-related, which is just a few moments' gentle stroll away from our building, around the other side of Clarence Dock.

Nathan takes my hand as the glass doors swish closed behind us, and we stroll slowly along the waterside, stopping to admire pieces of strategically placed street-art every few metres. As well as clever modern pieces, the decking is also strewn with old military artefacts such as cannons and rusty ships' anchors. They might be replicas—who knows? I like them.

Nathan points out the mews building where the museum keeps its stocky little jousting horses, hunting dogs and hawks. He shows me the tiltyard, where every day knights in full armour thunder up and down on their sturdy, specially imported little horses, slicing the heads off melons. Apparently I can watch the show from his bedroom window—if I can drag myself out of bed.

Once inside, we make our way to our table, which is shared with eight other couples, all colleagues and business associates of Nathan. He introduces me as his girlfriend, a musician and teacher. He didn't consult me on it beforehand, but I decide I like that self-image, especially the girlfriend bit. One or two intrigued eyebrows are raised around the table—clearly these people, who know him well, did not expect him to arrive with a romantic entanglement in tow.

I wonder briefly who else he might have brought if I hadn't shown up at Black Combe, but quickly dismiss that thought. Frankly, I don't care. I *am* here, with him. And I'm out to enjoy myself. So the conversation flows, his associates make me welcome, and I am easily able to join in with intelligent comments. Well, what else am I good at? Intelligence is my middle name.

The food is okay—not desperately wonderful, but good enough, in a fine dining meets mass catering sort of way. We have crab fishcakes and a green salad to start, followed by a chicken dish with a tomato and garlic sauce. The vegetables are served nouveau cuisine style, in little fancy shapes on a crescent-shaped side plate. The pudding is my favourite—a smooth, creamy orange-flavoured mousse served in a wine glass. I tuck in, then scrounge Nathan's off him too when he lets slip that he doesn't have much of a sweet tooth. I love desserts, and don't like to see one go to waste, or be less than properly appreciated. So I help out.

Throughout the meal Nathan constantly grins at me, obviously enjoying himself as much as I am, and his arm spends most of the evening looped around the back of my chair, across my shoulders. I have no illusions about what my main purpose is on this trip, but Nathan does seem inclined to enjoy my company as well. I find myself leaning my head against his shoulder, and his hold tightens slightly, approving.

After the food come the awards. Nathan's team wins second prize in its category, which he seems pleased enough with. The highest honour goes to a multinational who has created some sort of 'garden in the city' development — a quirky sort of place offering residents the chance to buy allotments as well as an apartment and a parking space, and even funky little garden sheds. Everyone claps enthusiastically, the audience awash with smiles, dinner jackets and glittery frocks.

I notice most of the other women are wearing black — plenty of sparkle, of course, but still black. I feel somewhat conspicuous in bright emerald green, and I wonder if Nicola deliberately selected a dress that would make me stand out rather than blend it. And if so, was she acting on Nathan's instructions? Certainly, he seems to like my look, insists it is unique, that I am beautiful. When he's not being intimidating he can be perfectly charming. He says some really kind things to me, really often, and even though I'm not fooled — after all, he's made his intentions absolutely clear and this is all part of his strategy for getting me into his bed, or wherever — it's still nice. He makes me feel good. Most of the time. I seem to recall he said I had a beautiful bottom, just before he laid into my bum with a ruler. I shift in my seat, still wincing as I remember how much that hurt, and the muscles way down in my belly clench as I remember the 'reward' for my compliance, the wonderful orgasm that followed.

After the presentations, we dance. Nothing too elaborate or ambitious, just a bit of gentle swaying to smooch music, his arms loosely around me and my face leaning into his chest. We spend a peaceful, sensuous half-hour, and I am intensely aware of his body under my hands, his hard, muscular male body so unlike mine.

By mutual, unspoken consent we amble over to the bar and perch on high stools, me sipping a white wine spritzer and him with a bottle of Bud. His black bow tie is open and hanging loose now we've reached the wind-down part of the evening, his top button undone. But still he looks absolutely gorgeous, his sexy smile and dark eyes promising much more fun still to come.

My stomach is fluttering with excitement, anticipation. And apprehension, because I know he probably has something else in store too, something more...challenging, to be endured to whet his appetite—or mine? I'm really not sure now. I hope it won't involve spanking me again—my still tender bum really is in no shape for that treatment twice in the same day—but ultimately, I doubt I'll have any say in it.

Placing the empty beer bottle on the bar, Nathan turns to me, his head to one side, his eyes dark, passion-filled.

"Time to go, Eva." He holds out his hand, and I take it.

* * * *

We arrive back at Nathan's apartment, arm in arm, having made many, many stops along the route home for deep, arousing kisses. I doubt there's a doorway, wall or seat anywhere between here and the Armouries that we haven't graced with our sensual presence. It took us a lot longer to get back than the outward journey took.

The apartment door clicks shut, locking behind us, and Nathan shrugs off his dinner jacket, then drops it over the back of the settee. Going over to the kitchen worktop, Nathan picks up my discarded knickers from earlier, dangling them from his index finger. "Could you wear these now, do you think?"

"Yes, I think I could."

He nods, smiling briefly, passing me the handful of lace. "Good. That's my bedroom" — he indicates with his head which door is his — "I'll be a few minutes, and when I come in I'd like you to be wearing these, and nothing else. Is that okay, Miss Byrne?"

'Miss Byrne' again. There's a definite pattern emerging here. 'Miss Byrne' means either intense pain or intense pleasure. I know that when he's in this mood he will demand an answer. I supply it with a brief nod, and head for his bedroom door.

His room is bigger than the guest room, furnished in a masculine style with solid wood and dark leather. The king-size bed dominates the middle of the room. The duvet is black with narrow white stripes, and the curtains match it. The pillow cases are black. The carpet is dark grey, deep and thick. I kick off my gold sandals, sink my toes into the pile. Without further thought, I drop my gold chain belt alongside the sandals, and the dress follows.

Remembering my instructions, I dutifully remove my bra and slip the panties back on, before walking gingerly over to a chest at the foot of the bed. Kneeling in front of it, I slowly lift the lid. Even before I open the chest I know what I'm going to find in there, but still I'm chilled at the sight of so many whips, canes, leather straps, ropes, tape and other bondage paraphernalia, as seen earlier on that wonderful website, but now here, in the flesh. *Oh, Jesus, what have I let myself in for?*

Those were just pictures. These are real. And they are meant to be used on me. They *will* be used on me—that's why I'm here. And I already know first-hand how much this is going to hurt. My hands are shaking as I close the lid. In an attempt to calm myself, I drop my head down onto my arms, folded over the flat, cool oak of the lid, closing my eyes and concentrating on breathing in and out, slowly.

"You've been exploring, I see, Miss Byrne. And have you made your selection? Do you have a weapon of choice?"

I jump sharply, startled. I didn't hear him come in. He is crouching behind me, at my eye level, and puts out his hand to steady me as I spin around. Standing, he draws me to my feet, and kisses me lightly on the lips before slowly walking around me, his gaze raking up and down my body.

He stops behind me and hooks his thumbs into the elastic at the top of my panties, gently drawing them down to reveal my buttocks, still bearing the raised red stripes. I am unable to prevent my wince as he touches me, and squeeze my buttocks together in some form of ineffective self-defence at the light brush of the backs of his fingers over my tender skin, tracing the marks left by his earlier attentions.

He has removed his shirt, and the top button of his dress trousers is undone. His feet are bare. His chest is lean, sharply contoured, the washboard abdomen clearly visible above his waistband. Obviously a man who works out, or leads an otherwise very active life.

Compared to his physical perfection, and despite all his compliments and apparent approval earlier, I feel desperately self-conscious, keenly aware of my lack of natural curves, angular body, small breasts.

I know better now than to try to cover myself, so I stand still, my briefs lowered to let him study my bum, bearing his scrutiny and hoping his courtesy and kindness from earlier in the evening might extend to this situation. In all our sexual encounters so far, his normal, playful, lighthearted, charming personality has seemed to change the instant he laid his hands on me. He is unpredictable, intimidating, arrogant, forceful. And utterly wonderful.

Gently pulling my underwear back into position, he comes to stand at the side of me, his left palm still spread over my bottom, the knuckles of his right hand idly grazing the underside and tip of my breast as he leans in to bury his face in my hair.

His murmur is low, sensual. "Miss Byrne, you are a truly beautiful woman."

Relief washes over me. *Thank God.*

Straightening, he gently removes the pins and Damien's wooden claw from my hair, letting the copper and amber length of it fall across his hands, down my back. "I forgot to mention that I will always want your hair down when we are together. Please make sure of that in future, Miss Byrne." I nod dumbly, caught like a rabbit in headlights as his dark gaze captures mine.

"You're shivering. Are you cold?" I shake my head, not able to break eye contact with him. "Scared, then?" I hesitate, not sure what I am allowed to say, but for once he doesn't press me.

His eyes are warm, his voice gentle, reassuring. "Don't be afraid of me, Eva. Nothing's going to happen unless you agree. This afternoon was hard on you, Miss Byrne, I know that. And you're still a little sore, I gather?" He is lightly caressing my bottom. I nod. "Thought so. Just a little gentle fucking tonight, then. That suit you?"

I stare at him, wide-eyed, intensely relieved. My knees start to give way and he catches me, easily lifting me and dropping me lightly on his bed. After falling down beside me, he effortlessly rolls me onto my back and kisses me deeply, sensually, his tongue exploring my mouth. I tunnel my hands through his over-long hair as it flops forward, my tongue needing no invitation to join in the dance. He rolls, and I find myself on top, the aggressor, kissing him, plunging my tongue into his mouth. He is holding my hair back, combing his hands through it before sliding them down to my shoulders, my back, my hips. We roll again, and now I'm back underneath.

After a few moments of mindless kisses, his touch gliding up and down my body, smoothing quickly over my breasts, my hips, the sides of my legs, he takes my wrists in one of his hands and pins them above my head. Leaning over me, raised on one elbow, he nuzzles my nose with his.

"Gentle fucking doesn't mean no kinky stuff at all, Miss Byrne. I'm going to tie you to the bed. Okay?"

"Why? I'm not going anywhere." My earlier apprehension is back, my voice weak, breathy.

"Don't look so worried, Miss Byrne. And no frowning…" I make a conscious effort to straighten my face, and he grins knowingly. "You'll love this. Trust me."

Before I can respond he leans over me, reaching under the pillow to pull out a restraint of some sort. I only glimpse it for a moment, but it appears to be a strap about two feet long, with a leather, buckled 'bracelet' at either end. Swiftly he loops it around through the wooden slats in the headboard before cuffing first one of my hands, then the other. He fastens the buckles tightly around my wrists. It's not painful, and I can still move, but my arms are raised above my head and I feel helpless. I guess that's the plan.

Lying alongside me, leaning up on one elbow, he looks his fill. He strokes my breasts, my belly, before hooking his thumb in the waistband of my panties.

"You're looking damn good, Miss Byrne. I don't think we need these anymore, do we?" Glancing down at my pretty green and pink briefs, he looks back at me, one eyebrow raised. "I'm going to take them off. Okay?" Not waiting for an answer, he draws them down. "Lift your feet, Miss Byrne," he whispers, and I do. Nathan slips the briefs past my ankles and tosses them on the floor with the rest of my clothes. I realise this is the first time he has seen me totally nude, and I lie still, waiting for whatever might be coming next.

He combs his fingers lightly through my pubic hair. "A natural redhead, Miss Byrne. I knew that, but still, this is so gorgeous..." Turning briskly, he pulls a couple of pillows from the top of the bed. Then, lifting my hips, he pushes the pillows underneath me to raise my bum from the bed.

Then he is on me again, his elbows either side of my head as he kisses me deeply. He is lying on top of me—not heavily, since he's supporting his weight on his elbows—but he's between my legs and I can feel his erection through his pants, the fabric of his clothing rough against my sensitive, swollen pussy.

"You wanted me naked when I fuck you, I seem to recall, Miss Byrne. This is our first time so I'm happy to oblige, just this once." Rolling to one side, he unzips his pants and pushes them to his ankles. After kicking them off, he quickly disposes of his boxers too, a rather fetching shade of pale blue. He stands up, glancing down at me and letting me look my fill at him, before he strolls casually around the head of the bed, out of my line of sight. I hear a drawer open, then close again, and he is back, three condoms in his hand. He tosses them onto the pillow beside my head. *Three! Wow.*

"Be prepared, Miss Byrne." He grins as he comes back to lie beside me.

He is fully erect, enormous. His penis is thick, veined, and the head smoothly glistening with pre-cum. I know I am staring. I can't help it. He's magnificent, and so damned big. I'm absolutely sure that there's no way he's going to fit inside me. No way. I won't survive it.

With his unerring powers of observation, he knows what I am thinking. Turning my face towards his with his hand, he kisses me lightly. "Trust me, you'll be fine. And I'll make this so good for you, Eva…"

I lie still, closing my eyes, willing myself to relax. I have his promise. I know he won't let me down.

He leans over me and lowers his head to softly take my nipple in his mouth, lightly sucking. I arch up, gasping with pleasure. Inexperienced as I am, I know all about this. And this is so, so good…

He increases the pressure, just slightly, and repeats the treatment on my other nipple. I groan, writhing under him. He gently rakes his fingers through my pubic hair, twisting the light amber curls around his fingers, teasing, playing. I'm desperate for him to touch me, really touch me. My legs are open, and I spread them farther, wider, inviting...

His touch is featherlight as he slides his fingers over my clitoris just slightly, briefly nudging it, enough to kindle my awareness and promise much more, before slipping one long, gentle finger inside me. My hips shoot up off the bed—I am in absolute ecstasy. I think I might have cried out. I wriggle, trying to increase the pressure, my clit quivering for attention. He catches my eye for a moment, smiling softly, before sliding down my body to dip his tongue into my navel. He withdraws his finger from my vagina, wet and creamy with my juices, and spreads the natural lubrication all over my vulva. The caress is wonderful, but still I want him inside me and I give a small, inarticulate cry of disappointment, of loss, only to shudder with delight as he quickly shifts his position so his head is between my legs. I realise what he is intending to do a brief moment before his lips close around my clit and he flicks the engorged, desperate little nub with his tongue.

I scream, pulling against the straps restraining my hands, shocked at the intimacy of this, drowning in pleasure.

"Nathan, please, you can't... *I* can't. That's too much..." I am lost in the intense pleasure of the moment. I never, ever could have imagined anything feeling as wonderful as this—so intense, so delicious. Ignoring my protests, he increases the pressure, but his tongue is soft, gentle still. He lightly grazes my clit with his teeth—*Jesus*! I stiffen, thrusting my hips forward, unable to breathe, desperate for more, climbing towards, what? The most powerful climax in my limited experience, no doubt. And it's very near.

He slips one, then two fingers back inside me, twisting them, spreading them inside my vagina to caress my internal walls and angling to reach that special spot, pressing, rubbing.

And I'm lost, spiralling up and outwards, fracturing in a shower of scorching sparks as every nerve in my body connects, centred on the exquisite burst of pleasure between my legs. I lose awareness of everything except the intense convulsions gripping my lower body, my nipples tingling, my whole body pulsing in delight. He knows what he's doing—he strokes and licks me continually whilst I writhe and moan, knowing instinctively how to stretch out the moment, draw every last gasp of delight out of me. The orgasm seems to last forever, all else forgotten, swept away on waves of selfish pleasure.

At last I lie still, spent and satisfied, eyes closed, breathing again. Dimly, I hear the sound of the condom foil being torn open, and the snap as he rolls the latex into place. He lies over me, my legs spread wide either side of his hips. I can feel his erection, huge and thick, brushing across my pubic hair briefly before he raises his hips slightly to position himself at my entrance. I feel the large head of his penis pushing into me, but still drunk with pleasure and boneless with satisfaction, I can't rouse myself enough to tell him what he needs to know. Now. That this is my first time, that he needs to go slowly, be gentle, let me adjust—

He thrusts forward, and I scream again, this time in agony as the pain slices through me, white-hot. He is huge, absolutely enormous, and he has filled me to the hilt. I know I am dying. I can't possibly survive this—he must have torn me in two.

He stiffens, goes still. My eyes are squeezed tightly shut, my jaw clenched in pain, my teeth grinding together. My instinct is to stay still, not move. I am paralysed. He fills me totally, and I am impossibly stretched — tense, fragile, ready to tear apart if either of us moves.

"Eva?" His voice is quiet, but I can hear the disbelief and I am mortified, humiliated. Found lacking in my inexperience. God, how could I have messed this up so badly?

"Eva, open your eyes, love. Look at me." He caresses my face, his lips gentle as he kisses me lightly. I open my eyes, and his are soft, dark with passion, and concern — for me?

"Do you want me to stop?"

Yes. No! No. The pain is subsiding, my body adjusting. "Please, give me a moment…"

"Okay, take your time, love." Then, "I'm so sorry. I should have been more gentle. I would have, if, well… I thought with you being on the pill, and so eager for…everything, that you, well…"

For once, the mighty Nathan is lost for words. That's a result.

"Why didn't you tell me?"

Why, indeed? I try to keep the pain from my voice as I gasp my answer. "I thought if you knew I was, was…"

"A virgin," he puts in helpfully.

"Yes, a virgin," I bury my face in his shoulder, gathering my thoughts, searching for reasons. I can't believe I'm lying here under him, his massive cock deep inside me while both of us struggle not to move a muscle. And we're actually having a sensible conversation. Well, nearly sensible — I've yet to come up with a good answer.

There is only one answer. And given our current circumstances, I figure I've nothing to lose now. I take a deep breath and spill it.

"I didn't think you'd want me. If you knew I had no experience, nothing to offer you. And I thought maybe you wouldn't be able to tell, especially after your fingers, and that vibrator, and…everything…" My voice tails off. I'm embarrassed, humiliated by my own naïvety. "And I thought maybe I could learn fast. I am a fast learner." *Well, that's the truth.*

He groans, dropping his forehead onto the pillow beside mine, then turning his face to nuzzle my hair.

"Sweetheart, you should have told me. I could have really hurt you. Holy fuck, when I think of the things I've said to you, what I've done to you already. Christ… You must think I'm a heartless bastard." His voice is low, gentle, whispering into my ear.

God, I think I could love this man…

"You already have hurt me, several times." Despite my words, I am joking now, feeling lighter, more confident. He knows what a useless lover I am, and he's still here. Apologising to me instead of the other way around.

"But I've never hurt you by accident, before now…"

"I've ruined everything? I'm sorry." *God, what an idiot I am.*

"Not entirely ruined, I'd say. My ego is battered. I usually manage a lot more finesse than this. But I guess I can survive it if you can…"

"Your ego? What about my poor bum from your bloody ruler? I'd punch you in the ribs if my hands were free. That'd make us even."

Chuckling, he shakes his head. "Eva, once more, you absolutely amaze me." Raising himself onto his elbows again, he cradles my head in his hands, his eyes holding mine. "Are you sure you want to continue?" At my nod, he smiles widely. "Thank God for that. I would have tried, love, I would have really tried. But I think it might just kill me to stop now. Has the pain gone?"

"Yes," I whisper, nervous again.

"Okay, we'll take it slowly from now. Let me know if I hurt you again."

He slowly, gently, slides backwards, withdrawing from me. The friction against my inner walls feels strange, definitely not unpleasant. He stops, just the tip of his cock still inside me, then presses forward again, very slowly this time, filling me gradually, stretching me. I sigh. That glorious internal friction is even better now, and I take in his full length again. I can feel his cock nudging my cervix. It feels indescribably sexy, sensual, intimate. Fabulous. And it doesn't hurt.

He is very, very careful, as if afraid I might break, every tense, bunched muscle exerting control. "Okay?" he asks, his eyes holding mine. "Any more pain?"

I shake my head, unable to speak, just wanting to savour this new sensation. "Again?" he asks.

At my slight nod he repeats the action, the gentle withdrawal and slow thrust forward, and this time I can't contain my gasp of surprised pleasure. I could *really* get to like this.

"Is that good?" he asks softly. "More?"

"Yes. Yes, please."

His eyes never letting go of mine, he softly, sweetly sets up a rhythm. My moans of delight are swallowed by him as his mouth catches mine, his tongue plunging deep to mimic his cock, now smoothly stroking inside me. The feeling is beyond good, so intense, all the sweeter for being shared. His breathing is harsher now, his brow creased in concentration and pleasure. I start to soar, the now-familiar early tug of orgasm again gripping me. He rolls to take his weight on his right elbow, and using his left hand he reaches down between us, his fingers stroking my clit in time with the rhythm of his cock, now pumping firmly in and out of me. I grasp his shoulders, holding on for dear life, only now realising that at some point he has released my wrists from the leather straps and I am free to touch him, too. I'm thrusting and gyrating my hips to meet his, and I'm sobbing with need, pleading with him for more. *More what?*

He knows. "Do you want me to fuck you harder, Eva? Faster? Deeper?"

"Yes! Please, yes…"

He does, showing me no mercy now as he pounds into me, angling his thrusts so that his cock hits just the right spot, which he has so accurately located previously with his penetrating fingers. I am desperate, reaching for my climax.

"Come for me, angel," he whispers. "Come. Now."

The dam breaks, and I am once again soaring, joyously shattering, convulsing around him. With a curse, muffled as he buries his face in my hair, he shudders, jerking in his own climax. He thrusts once more, twice, then he is still. Instinctively, I brace myself to take his weight, but he quickly rolls onto his back, pulling me with him. I'm draped over him, sprawled across his body, his cock still deep inside me.

One by one, my senses return. I can hear — the only sound is our heavy breathing, slowly returning to normal. I can feel — his hand gently stroking my back, my bottom, no longer sore. If I open my eyes I can probably see, but that's too much trouble just now.

I feel incredible. And confused. Full of joy, certainly — elated, exulting in what has just happened, what I've managed to achieve, how bloody glorious it was. And I am desperately sad that it can only last a few weeks, then I'll go back to being lonely.

Lonely? Where did that come from? Am I lonely?

And I can hear one word in my head, going round and round as if on a loop. A familiar word, a name, spoken by a long-forgotten, always loved and always remembered voice.

'Angel'. My daddy.

Nathan breaks into my thoughts. "Well, Miss Byrne, that was quite a ride," he murmurs. "Hey, are you okay?" Tipping my face up with his fingers he sees the tears streaming down my cheeks. I hadn't realised I was crying, but now I can't seem to stop. Seems the floodgates didn't just apply to my orgasm.

I'm embarrassed again, not sure what's happening, why I'm feeling so emotional when I never have been before, over anything. Even when my father died I didn't really cry, just bottled up the aching loss and went back to my books. I've no idea how to start to deal with any of this. My instinct is to hide, so I jerk my chin away from his hand and bury my nose in his beautiful, sculpted chest, now sobbing uncontrollably as a lifetime's worth of pent-up emotion pours from me, spilling out onto this beautiful man. I vaguely expect meaningless words of comfort, more apologies, anything to stop me crying. But instead he just tightens his arms around me, saying nothing, holding me close while I let it all out.

When I am finally quiet, he gently eases me off him, disengaging. I had forgotten he was still there, deep inside me, and I do feel a sense of loss now, even though his erection had become distinctly less imposing. Rolling from the bed, he quickly removes the condom, and through my slitted eyes I see him tie the end in a knot, then quirk his lips at the bloodstains on the outside of it. Proof positive of my virginity. How could I have thought he'd be fooled for a moment?

He strides across the room, through a door into what I suppose must be the en suite. Yes—I hear a toilet flushing, running water, then he is back, carrying a box of tissues and a flannel. Sitting on the side of the bed, he pulls me, unresisting, into his lap. He gently wipes my face, first with tissues, then with the warm, damp flannel.

"I don't think you were crying because of me. Were you, Eva?" I shake my head. "Okay, good. So can you explain the tears?"

"No. I'm not sure. Maybe some of it..." My voice trails away as I try to put the pieces in order. Moments pass. He doesn't press me, just waits for me to be ready. I work it through in my head logically, as I always do, in that way I am usually so good at. Working out causal relationships, sequences, making sense of problems, finding solutions. And I am amazed, in awe at what I have discovered, about me, my memories, what I need. He has unlocked so much more than just my repressed sexuality. I say the one thing that makes sense to me.

"'Angel'. You called me 'angel'."

"Yes." He nods—I suppose remembering those moments just before he came—but says nothing more, giving no prompts, waiting for me to explain.

Sniffling into his chest, I draw a deep, shuddering breath and continue shakily. "My daddy was the only one to call me Angel. I was...reminded of him. I loved him. Very much."

"You miss him? Still? It's been fifteen years since he died."

I stiffen in his arms. "How did you know that?" I am shocked, genuinely stunned. Has he been checking up on me? How much more does he know?

"You told me, that first night you showed up at Black Combe. When I made fun of your name. You told me he died when you were seven."

Ah, right. He has an amazing memory for details. The way I do.

"I'm glad I put you in mind of someone you loved. But, sweetheart, you have to know my attitude towards you is a long way from being fatherly..." He is grinning, teasing me again. How sweet he can be when he wants to be, and he knows just what I need, how to get me through this.

I stumble on, trying to explain, to make it make sense to him too. "I'm not used to...anything like this. This has been a hell of a day for me. What happened this afternoon, in your office, was so overwhelming. And then I've had such a lovely evening. And now, here, we've... I mean, I've waited so long for a man to want to... And you were wonderful. Brilliant."

"Ah, my ego is restored. And, honey, let me tell you, you've been hanging around the wrong men if no one ever offered to fuck you before. Still, my gain..." Suddenly switching tack, he goes straight for the jugular. "Tell me about your dad. What was he called?"

I hesitate, but hell, we've got this far. "Charles. Charlie. His name was Charlie Byrne. And—I haven't said his name out loud, not even talked about him, since I was seven."

"Well, we'll talk about him now, then. How did he die?"

"He crashed his plane."

"His plane?"

"He was an RAF pilot. He died when a routine training manoeuvre went wrong."

"Shit, that must have been a hell of a shock for you. For your mum too."

I need to think about that for a moment. I don't recall my mother grieving overmuch for him. Eventually, I tell him, "They didn't get on. He was...not exactly a faithful husband. She was very angry with him, always angry. And just before he crashed they argued. They always argued, but that last time was really bad. Brutal. She said she'd had enough, that we were leaving. I listened from my bedroom in our RAF bungalow, angry myself because she'd never asked me if I wanted to leave. Then he was gone. He came into my room and kissed me goodnight, called me his angel, went off to work as usual and never came home again." Done with crying, at least for tonight, I draw in a huge breath, then let it out slowly, remembering. "I've never told anyone any of this before. No one ever asked."

"Well, I'm asking now. Your dad sounds like a wonderful guy."

"My mother doesn't think so."

"Maybe not. Not back then, anyway. But you should ask her again. She might tell you something different now, now that the anger has gone. Where did he die? Were you abroad?"

"No. He was based in Scotland at that time. I think he's buried near Dundee."

"You think? Haven't you been to his grave? What about at his funeral?"

"I didn't go. I was angry too, because he left me. Even though we were going to leave him, it seems. So I didn't go. I didn't cry. I just got on with my life. We had to leave our bungalow soon after that, and Mum and I went to live in London. We were okay—my mum had her RAF pension and some other money she inherited from him. Quite a lot, I suppose, because she never needed to get a job. And we never talked about him anymore. *I* never talked about him again. Until now."

He is silent for a few moments, just holding me. Then he kisses my hair. His next words astonish me. "Lots of unfinished business there, I think, my little Eva. How about if we find out where that grave is and go there, say goodbye properly. Maybe your mum would like to come too."

My mum! I'm here, naked in his bed, my virginity just a memory, and he's talking about going on a family outing with my mother. I can't help it—I giggle. "I'm not sure my mum would like you very much."

He is affronted. "Me? What's not to like?"

"Well, it might be your whips, your chains, your skill with a ruler…?"

"Well, let's not bother her with all that, then. Which reminds me, Miss Byrne…" *Ah, I'm Miss Byrne again, lovely…* "We have unfinished business."

He doesn't wait for a response before I find myself facedown on the bed. He kneels behind me, lifting my bum up to pull me onto all fours, and slides his wonderful, skilful fingers deep into me, testing my wetness, my readiness. Once more I hear the snap of the foil packet tearing as he extracts condom number two from his collection. A few seconds later, gently opening me with both of his thumbs, he positions the head of his cock between the lips of my vagina, and I brace instinctively. Sensing my hesitation, he caresses my bum, steadying me, reassuring.

"I won't hurt you this time, Miss Byrne. But please do feel free to scream anyway."

Chapter Seven

He didn't, and I did.

Practice makes perfect, they say, and the second time did seem pretty much perfect to me. I came three times, twice as he stoked my clit in time with his firm, controlled thrusting, and the third time as he raised the pace still further, dropping any attempt at control as he attended to his own needs. He stiffened behind me, grasping my buttocks hard to hold me still as he pounded inside me. I trembled as orgasm took me once more, but was still aware when he jerked, his body clenching as mine was. He muttered something along the lines of 'Holy fuck, angel', and I felt the heat of his semen filling the condom. It was absolutely wonderful, magical, exhausting.

Afterwards we lay still, no words needed, me tucked up with my back snuggled against Nathan's chest, his arm loosely around my hips. We slept.

Now bright daylight is flooding the room, the curtains at the floor to ceiling, panoramic windows opened wide to let in the morning. I am alone, lying in his huge bed, stretching like a contented cat, still purring from yesterday's intensely satisfying initiation into the art of lovemaking. Except he would call it 'gentle fucking'. What's in a name? It *was* gentle. And it was fucking good.

Nathan is not in the room, and I listen for any sign of where he is. Nothing, no sounds of running shower or flushing loo from the en suite, just silence. Disorientated, I glance at the clock—just turned ten. I guess it was around two by the time he finally let me sleep, and I've been out cold for eight hours solid. How glorious. I haven't slept so well since my first night at Black Combe, and maybe not even then.

Refreshed, eager to face the day—and Nathan—I slip out of bed and walk, nude and completely unconcerned, across to the en suite. My natural modesty would usually have curbed such exhibitionism, but today things seem different. I'm less inhibited somehow, and we're so high up, in any case—the only way anyone would see in would be from a passing aeroplane. I turn on the shower and step in, leaning my hands and forehead against the tiled wall as the warm multi-jets hit me from all directions, the water streaming down my back, belly, my breasts, my hair, my legs. I relax, rolling my shoulders, my neck.

Then I jump as warm, wet, soapy hands reach around me to caress my breasts. My alarm is short-lived as passion once again takes over. Nathan is behind me, also nude, and sharing my shower.

Another first for me, and this seems incredibly intimate. Oddly so, given all we have done, all we have already shared. I lean back against him, dropping my head to one side to let him nuzzle my neck, whisper in my ear about how beautiful I am, how sexy, how gorgeous, and all the wicked, forbidden things he intends to do to me. I tremble, anticipating.

He soaps me all over, kneeling behind me to wash my legs, my bottom, even inserting the tip of his slick, soapy finger into my anus, just slightly—enough to make me jump and gasp before he withdraws it. "Just testing, making sure you're paying attention, Miss Byrne. Turn around."

I do, so he can wash my front. This takes a long time, since he carefully washes every fold and crease, every throbbing inch of me before kneeling in front of me and nudging my thighs apart with his shoulders. He rinses the soap off then leans in to lick the moisture away, only succeeding in making me wetter still. Clinging to his shoulders, I come, helpless, boneless. I would have slid to the tiles below my feet but for his arm across my stomach, pinning me upright against the wall of the shower. When he's sure I can take my own weight again, he stands to wash my breasts, squeezing my nipples between his slick fingers until I groan with pleasure and pain.

Turning me so I have my back to him again, he soaps my hair, massaging the lather into my scalp. Never have I felt so…so cherished. I was a small child when I last had my hair washed, unless you count Damien and the other nameless hairdressers who've battled with my hair over the years, but that was different—that was business. This is sensuous, delightful, intimate.

I close my eyes to savour the delicious sensations, once more leaning forward to prop myself up against the tiles, lost in contentment. Nathan rinses the lather out, then finger-combs conditioner through the long, curling strands. Then, the conditioner still in, he takes a comb from somewhere and gently de-tangles the smooth, silky waves. Eventually he rinses the conditioner away then turns me to face him again, this time to take my face between his palms and kiss me. Not my mouth this time, not immediately. He drops tender kisses over my eyes, my eyebrows, my ears, my jaw, my chin, before finally, at last, taking my mouth and plunging his tongue deep. Only after long, dragging minutes does he finally come up for air.

"Are you hungry, Miss Byrne? Can I interest you in any breakfast?"

"I-I think I might... No, I..."

"We've got bacon, cereals, croissants. Coffee goes without saying. After I've fucked you senseless again, obviously."

Obviously.

* * * *

It's nearly eleven by the time I am finally seated on a stool against the kitchen worktop, one of Nathan's shirts covering me. I rummaged through my bags from yesterday's shopping expedition for some fresh underwear, and I can already feel the moisture pooling in them as his excess semen slides from me. I am learning fast that being well fucked twice within an hour of waking up leaves a sticky mess behind. I do so like this mess.

We had a serious talk earlier, about condoms. To use or not to use — that was the question. Given my obvious lack of previous partners, and the fact that I already have contraception sorted out, that only left Nathan's not exactly chaste sexual history to bother us. He has regular medicals and volunteered access to the records. I declined, satisfied with the offer. So now, we're bareback. Hence the mess.

I wrap my hands around a mug of weak coffee, just the way I like it. A warm croissant's buttery aroma wafts towards me. I break a piece off, nibble it. I don't much like jam, so I prefer it plain.

Nathan, wearing just sweatpants, shoves wholemeal bread into the toaster, then pours strong, black coffee down his throat. Radio Two is chuntering away in a corner somewhere, the sound just wallpaper, blending hardly noticed into the background Nathan's copy of Friday's *Guardian* is still open on the dining table, where he had obviously been reading it just before hearing me in the shower and taking an interlude to join me. We seem every inch the perfect, companionable, compatible couple, pottering around the breakfast bar.

"Your shopping's arrived." Nathan nods towards the table, where I see an anonymous-looking, brown cardboard box perched on a chair. About a foot wide by about eighteen inches deep, and a couple of feet long, it looks harmless enough—could contain anything. I can't think what 'shopping' is still to arrive, though. Harvey Nicks sent everything across, as far as I can tell. I frown, puzzled, trying to think what might have been missing from my purchases.

"You're frowning again, Miss Byrne. And I think you know what happens now. Come here."

Startled, I can only stare as he walks casually, confidently across the room to seat himself at the table, taking a chair next to my mysterious parcel. "What? W-what do you mean?"

"You know exactly what I mean. Come here, Miss Byrne. And bend over my knee, please." His tone is even, quiet and absolutely unrelenting. I have enough presence of mind to realise he has nothing in his hand, but I am rooted to my spot by the worktop.

"Don't make me come and get you, Eva. Come here. Now."

I drag my feet across the floor, my eyes caught by his gaze, until I am standing a couple of feet from him. "What do you want me to do?" I whisper.

"Lie face down across my knees." Stiffly, shaking, I do as I am told. He pulls me forward, positioning me so my bottom is directly over his left knee, my stomach over his right knee and my upper body dropping forward towards the floor. My hair, still loose, falls around my face, pooling on the floor. I use my hands to try to steady myself.

"Don't try to push yourself up, Eva. I'll tell you when we're done. Keep still." He lifts the shirt to my waist and gently pulls my briefs down to my knees. I idly note that I never seem able to keep a pair on for more than a few minutes at a time.

His right hand firmly across my back, holding me in place, he rests his left palm on my left buttock, idly curling his fingers, fondling the soft flesh. I lie there, a little bit terrified and a lot excited. My bottom is quivering now, tensed, and I wait. "Are you ready, Miss Byrne?" Yes—yes, I am. I tell him so, and the first blow falls.

Sharp, stinging, with a loud slap that shocks me nearly as much as the sudden pain, the palm of his hand connects with my bottom. Hard. I squeal, wait for the next blow. But it doesn't come. Not yet. Instead, he strokes the pain away, gently caressing my stinging buttock until I unclench, relaxed, ready once more. He lifts his palm and spanks me again, maybe a little harder this time. The sound of the slap reverberates around the room and I jerk with pain, crying out. As before, he soothes, strokes, caresses until I relax, lying loosely across his thighs, ready and waiting.

Another blow lands and I cry out again, my eyes starting to tear up now as the sharp, stinging pain shoots through me. I squeeze my eyes shut, clench my teeth as well as my butt and wait for the spanking to continue.

"You seem very tense, Miss Byrne. We need you to relax. Open your legs."

Dazed, I do as I am told. With questing fingers, he probes between my buttocks, sliding farther to dip into my moist vagina before circling my clit. I can't help it—I gasp, moan with pleasure as I am treated to the most erotic experience I could ever imagine. And my imagination is certainly getting a workout lately. He strokes me almost to orgasm before suddenly lifting his hand and administering another hard slap to my bottom. This time I scream out loud in shock, pain, frustration. Then his hand is back between my legs, working its magic on my swollen clit. I'm so wet it's obscene.

This time, surely he's not going to…

I reach greedily towards orgasm, wriggling against his legs, moaning as he works my clit into a frenzy of throbbing need. Then he stops. Before I can protest, the fifth slap across my unresisting, helpless bottom sends me jerking, spinning into orbit as I shake with the intensity of my climax.

He strokes me, caresses my smarting behind until I am still, quiet, complete. Then he gently pulls my briefs back up and draws me upright, then turns me to sit in his lap while he eases my face against his shoulder, combing his fingers through my tangled hair. "Was that okay, angel?" he asks me gently, stroking my hair, nuzzling the top of my head.

I can only nod, not able to speak yet, stunned by my reaction. How did he make me come by spanking me, hurting me, scaring me?

"Your shopping..." He nudges the chair next to him with his foot, making the parcel wobble. "You should open it."

Sitting up, I try to concentrate, reach for the parcel, then turn it around so I can read the address label. Sure enough, it's addressed to me, Eva Byrne, at Nathan's address here in Leeds. But I'm puzzled, confused. "I didn't buy anything else. Are you sure it's mine?"

"Certainly is. It's your Internet shopping from yesterday."

I jerk back from it. He catches me before I topple us both, chuckling at my alarm. "There's some nice stuff in there, Eva. You chose it yourself. I'll get you some scissors." After pushing me to my feet, he crosses to the kitchen units and fishes in a drawer for a pair of kitchen scissors. I stand, my eyes riveted to the innocent-looking brown parcel that I now know contains dizzying extremes of pain and pleasure.

And it's here so soon. I'd sort of assumed I'd have a few days, at least, to get accustomed to this, this...arrangement. To practise a bit more before getting into the really rough stuff.

Nathan's chuckle is soft, sexy. "We've been practising." *Oh, Christ, I said what I was thinking out loud again. That could be a dodgy habit — I need to watch that.* "And I paid extra for next day delivery. Didn't want to keep you waiting, Miss Byrne. You might have been bored."

Fat chance of that.

He hands me the scissors, nodding towards the parcel. Obediently I set to, slicing through the shiny brown parcel tape. The top flaps spring loose, and a stream of polystyrene balls spill out to dance crazily across the dining room floor. Ignoring the mess, I tentatively reach in. First to emerge is my sweet little U-shaped vibrator, discreetly packaged in a little pink and white cardboard box. 'Batteries not included.' Oh, dear...

"I have plenty of batteries, Eva." *Yes, you would.*

Next out is a cane. Less happy to see that, I lay it on the table top next to my vibrator.

"You'll come to love that too, Eva. Just takes a bit more getting used to. Like being spanked."

I blush, remembering what he's just done to me. Absentmindedly, I rub my bum.

"Let me do that for you." He pushes my hand aside and he strokes my bottom, under the shirt, over my panties. "Your gorgeous, sexy little arse is going to be so busy today. What else is in there?"

Not scared now, not really—more nervously anticipating—I pull out the feather tickler and suede flogger, laying them next to the cane.

"Ah, Miss Byrne, how little you know..."

Then comes a spanking crop. The pressure on my bum increases—Nathan slides his hand under the lace on the back of my panties and I wince without thinking, but add the crop to our collection calmly enough, glancing at him over my shoulder. He is smiling, obviously enjoying my nervousness.

I pull out what looks like a bracelet of shiny metal beads. I don't remember ordering this—maybe it's a free gift or something. I turn the short string over in my hands, not taking it out of the clear plastic covering, and can see the end bead, the largest one, has a small switch on it. And a tiny flap fastened by a screw. Another battery compartment?

"Anal beads," he whispers into my ear. "Fabulous sensation. You'll love them."

"But, how do I…? How do they get in my—?"

"That's my department, sweetheart. And trust me, I'll make sure they get where they need to be."

"That's got to hurt."

"Not if it's done right. With a lot of lubricant. The lubricating's half the fun. And when I fuck you, good and hard, with those in your arse, you'll think you've died and gone to heaven. I promise."

Dear God! My face flaming scarlet, I stick my nose back into the brown parcel and retrieve the last two smaller boxes. One contains my nipple clamps, complete with vibrating bullets. The picture of the busty model on the outside of the box, the mauve nipple clamps gaily swinging from her larger than life nipples, is a bit daunting and I can't help a sympathetic glance down at my inoffensive pair of modest boobs. I don't dare cast a glance Nathan's way. I just know he is also staring at my chest and I only hope he's not comparing me to the picture. It's all right for her—she clearly makes a decent living demonstrating nipple clamps. I'm just a novice.

The final package is unmarked, just a small, brown cardboard box. I open it to find seven brightly coloured plastic objects inside, ranging from about three and a half to five inches long, the smallest about the width of a thumb, the largest maybe three times as thick. They are blunt at one end and have a little ring at the other end, attached to a moulded plastic stem about two inches long. I am baffled. I certainly didn't order these, and have no idea what they might be for.

Always helpful, Nathan has the answer. "Butt plugs, love. One for every colour of the rainbow. Or every day of the week. We'll start small and work up to this bad boy." He takes the largest one from the box and tests the weight and size in his hand. "Hmm, your tight little virgin butt might need some persuading, but we'll get there. Like I say, plenty of lube." Looking up, he catches my stunned expression and smiles wickedly. "Hey, you might have noticed, my cock's thicker than this. And I do intend to fuck your arse very soon, so please take that look off your face, Miss Byrne, before I'm tempted to spank you again."

Speechless, I stare at him. I seem to stare a lot these days. My mother would not be amused, as she has always told me it's rude to stare. I am beginning to appreciate that all things are relative.

Leaning against the table, his hips braced on the edge, Nathan gently turns me in his arms, loosely looping his fingers together at the small of my back. His chest is bare, beautiful, sculpted. My nose is about level with his flat, hard nipples, and I have a sudden urge to lean forward and flick one with my tongue. So I do. Fair's fair. He's done the same—and much, much more—to mine. I tip my head back, grin up at him. He is shaking his head, his smile gentle, amused. And tender.

A sudden, unexpected thought strikes me. "Am I allowed to touch you? Do subs do that?"

Head cocked to one side, he smiles at me. "It depends. Not as a rule, I suppose. But yes, I would like you to, if that's what you want right now. Feel free." He leans back, his hands extended, palms out, in a gesture of invitation. I don't need to be asked twice.

I run my palms up and down his hard chest, exploring. To the best of my recollection—and I do have an exceptionally good memory—this is absolutely the first time I've had my hands on anyone—anyone at all, male or female—and I am entirely fascinated. Nathan's chest is smooth. He has a sprinkling of chest hair, but he's not as hairy as so many others seem to be. I had sort of assumed all men were alike. His nipples are small, flat, hard little nubs, and he shivers when I rub them.

"Does that feel like it does for me?" I am intrigued. Could it be the same?

"Probably, a bit. But yours are very sensitive." He starts to reach for me but I step back, defying him. At his raised eyebrow I hurry to explain, plead my case before he takes over, dominating me again. "Please, you said I could touch you. Let me. Let me touch all of you. Please."

He hesitates a moment, then drops his hands, nods. I continue.

I run my palms up his ribs, feeling the hard bones of his ribcage below the skin and muscle. His arms are firm, the biceps tight, bulging slightly—strong, certainly, but not pumped up. I remember how easily he lifted me, swung me around, that night back at Black Combe when we went out stargazing. I lay my cheek against his chest, listen to his steady, slow heartbeat, and wonder if I might be able to pep it up, just a bit. I slide my hand under the elasticated waistband of his sweatpants and he breathes in sharply, his posture stiffening. *Yes!*

I slide my fingers lower, combing through his pubic hair just as he trailed his fingers through mine yesterday. He's already hard. His heavy, large erection nudges the back of my hand, but I ignore it. For now. I reach lower, cupping his balls, squeezing lightly. They are heavier than I imagined, and he groans as I roll them in my palm, his head thrown back, his arms braced on the table. "Eva, please... Eva."

"What? What do you want me to do, Mr Darke?" Two can play that game.

I continue to stroke his balls very softly, very, very gently.

"Shit, Eva. You'll pay for this. Or your backside will..." he growls, his eyes glinting down at me. Intimidated, I start to pull my hand back. Have I gone too far? Overstepped my submissive role, before I even properly understand what it is? I start to apologise, but he grabs my wrist, my hand still in his pants. "Fuck it, Eva, just put your hand around my cock. Grip it. Hard."

I do as I'm told. It's big—my fingers can't quite close around it. And it's hard, solid, smooth and silky. "Run your hand up to the top, and slide your thumb around over the head," Nathan whispers hoarsely. "Please, Eva." I do as instructed, at the same time leaning in to drop kisses across his chest.

The head of his cock is wet. More moisture dribbles out onto my thumb. It's hot and slippery. And so tempting. Instinct taking over, I slide my hand up and down along the shaft. Each time I return to the top, I swipe my thumb around in the dewy moisture there, then spread it over the rest of him.

He is shuddering—this huge, intimidating man who has thrashed and spanked me and scared me half to death is shaking under my hand. Not stopping to think, to ask permission, I drop to my knees and pull his sweatpants down. Taking his penis between my hands, I angle it away from his body so that I can take it in my mouth. And I suck. Hard. Just like he does to my nipples and my clit, with such devastating results. Maybe I can...

"Jesus, Eva, that's so fucking good." His voice is low, a growl. And he's thrusting his hips, his cock going deeper, hitting the back of my throat. His hands are in my hair, but not holding me, not forcing my head forward. I can withdraw if I want. Encouraged, willing, I graze my teeth along the shaft, and swirl my tongue around the head, experimenting with the salty taste. *Not unpleasant.*

"Eva, if you don't fancy a mouthful of spunk, you need to stop. Now!"

There's no way I'm stopping now, or anytime soon. By way of answer I run my hands over his tight buttocks, pulling him closer before I slide my hand down to squeeze his balls from behind.

"God, you're a fun date, Eva," is his appreciative reply, groaned in a low, guttural rasp. Moments later, he squeezes my head tightly between his hands and holds me still at last, thrusting his cock once, twice, to the back of my throat before I feel and taste a gush of hot, salty semen. I swallow fast, to clear my mouth and throat, and breathe again.

Combing his fingers through my hair, he gently lifts my head, drawing his still-erect cock out of my mouth. He looks down at me, kneeling at his feet. No doubt that's the correct position for a sub...

Crouching, he smiles into my face before kissing me softly. "That was so damned good. Thank you. And you didn't have to finish with me in your mouth. But I'm glad you did."

Standing, he lifts me easily, carrying me back into the bedroom. "Now for some more fun. Are you ready to try out your new toys for grown-ups, Eva?"

Chapter Eight

Standing in the middle of Nathan's big bedroom, surrounded by his chunky, solid furniture, I glance around nervously, especially reluctant to go anywhere near the chest at the foot of the bed. I needn't have bothered worrying, as he goes striding back into the dining room for my new collection of erotica, then brings everything back in the large box, which he tosses onto the bed.

"You'll need your safe words, Eva. Do you remember what they are?"

"Why? I may not need safe words at all. I was okay yesterday. And again just now."

"Just now, I was only playing. And yesterday was yesterday, and still pretty mild. Today we ramp it up a bit. So safe words, Eva—what are they?"

His gaze is hard, steely, uncompromising. Gone is the playful lover of just a few minutes ago. I answer quietly, obediently, the perfect little fearful sub. "Red if I want you to stop, yellow to slow down, to be careful. Do you really think I'll need to use them?" There's a tremor in my voice. In moments I have gone from willing and eager sex kitten—*yes, me, sex kitten!*—to terrified sub, a knot of dread forming in my stomach as I realise he means it. He intends to hurt me, and by the sound of it he'll hurt me more than he did yesterday. I agree this morning was different—not serious. But the beating I received in his office yesterday was absolute agony, the pain was quite blinding.

My every instinct screams at me to run, and I know if I say I want to leave he'll drive me back to Black Combe without argument. But I'm still here, standing, waiting. Watching while he selects the spanking crop from the box. Holding it at both ends, he regards me seriously, intently. I gulp and back off.

He sees it and offers me a way out. "You don't have to go through with this, Eva. Do you want to back out of our deal? You can go back to Black Combe. Teach violin and walk the moors with Rosie and Barney, break in your new shoes and waterproof."

I'm frightened of what's in store here and now, but more scared by the emptiness of my future if I fail. I dread failure, the loneliness of losing this exciting, fabulous sensuality that he is unwrapping in me, the sparkling opportunity to discover insights, feelings, sensations that will last me a lifetime. I need this—it's that simple. So I answer firmly, with certainty.

"Yes, I want to do all that, at Black Combe. And this too." I lift my chin, ready. "I'm in."

He nods, smiles. "Excellent, Miss Byrne. Take off the shirt."

I do, hardly bothered anymore by my near nudity as I stand before him in just my lace briefs. My modesty and shyness do seem to have been beaten—or seduced—out of me, as he promised. I meet his gaze.

His eyes are warm, appreciative. He looks me up and down slowly.

"At the risk of repeating myself, your body is exquisite, Miss Byrne. You are one lovely woman. You take my breath away."

He comes to me, takes my face in his palms and kisses me lightly, touching his lips to my eyelids, my neck, and finally my lips before standing back. His gaze caresses my breasts, then his hands follow, slowly tracing the curved underside of each before trailing his fingers to the tips. Taking each of my nipples between his fingers and thumbs, he softly rolls them, delicately teasing them to swollen hardness.

"Should we use the nipple clamps today Miss Byrne? Or maybe save those for another time. Something to look forward to, for both of us..." He drops his hands, turns away.

Leaving me gulping in the middle of the room, he goes to the chest, opens it and takes out a metal bar about two feet long, with a leather strap at each end. "For your wrists, Miss Byrne. Please..."

Holding the restraint before me, he waits for me to place my wrists in the leather cuffs before tightening them. Then, while I hold my arms out stiffly in front of me, he grasps the metal bar and tugs me across the room. Glancing up, he pulls a metal ring on a chain from the ceiling. It's clearly spring-loaded because he fastens the metal rod securely to it and when he lets it go, my hands are raised above my head, my whole body pulled upright, onto my toes, then into the air.

I am suspended, my feet about a foot off the floor. I scream. My wrists hurt like hell for a moment as all my weight is suspended from them, but Nathan quickly slips his arm around me, taking my weight as he kicks a low stool under my feet so I can stand. Just about, on tiptoe.

"I keep forgetting how small you are..." he murmurs. "If you turn your hands you can hold onto the bar — might be more comfortable." His advice is helpful, as ever. I steady myself as best I can.

I'm shivering, but not with cold, nor fear now. I recognise this feeling — anticipation. My immobility is oddly empowering, and I realise that I felt a similar liberation last night as he tied my wrists to the bed. He's in control — as long as I let him be. But for now, I can relinquish responsibility and see what happens.

Nathan walks around to stand in front of me, his face now only an inch or so higher than mine. He kisses me again. "Safe words, Eva. Remember," he murmurs before turning to pick up a bottle of water from the floor behind him. He snaps the plastic top and offers me a drink.

"Your mouth is dry, Eva. Drink. Small sips." He holds the bottle to my lips. I drink greedily, only now realising how parched my body feels. "Enough?"

I nod, grateful. "Yes. Thank you."

"If you need more, tell me. And for fuck's sake, use the safe word if you need to. When you need to." With that, he turns away. He's behind me, but I hear his footsteps crossing the room, then coming back slowly, unhurried. "I'm going to blindfold you, Eva. Hold still."

Before I can react, he slips a blindfold over my eyes. All is pitch black. I'm disorientated at first, terrified I'll fall from my perch. "Please, I don't like it. Please take it off." My voice sounds desperate, trembling again and I start to panic, tugging against the restraints on my wrists, struggling to be free.

He steadies me, his hands at my waist, but he's unrelenting. "You'll get used to it. And the sensations will be so much more…intense. Be still, you won't fall. I'll tell you when to move."

A few seconds pass in silence. I struggle to regain my self-control, standing there in the dark with my arms stretched tightly above my head, unable to move, helpless. I'm beginning to appreciate that helplessness can have its own attractions, an appeal that I'd not dreamed of before, but this is still scary. I hope I don't disgrace myself, do something ridiculous like faint. Or pee myself. God, how embarrassing. Still, that'd show him, the heartless bastard. Despite my apprehension that image amuses me, sort of, and I manage a tremulous little almost-smile.

"Something amusing you, Miss Byrne?" His voice is low beside my ear, and I jump nervously as Nathan slips his thumbs into the waistband of my briefs. He pulls them down to my ankles. "Step out," he orders. Naturally, I do. Naked now, helpless and strangely free, I wait.

Suddenly something firm, supple, is trailed down my back, from between my shoulder blades to my bum, then down between my buttocks. It isn't painful, but it seems all the more menacing for its softness. I guess he is teasing me, stroking me with a whip of some sort. "What's that?" I whisper, arching my body away. "Please, if that's a whip, please just do it." I can't stand the tension, the waiting.

"There's no rush, Miss Byrne. This is about arousal, not punishment. Be patient." His voice is soft, tender almost, and he draws the whip around to the front, trailing it over my breasts, my belly. Sliding it between my legs. I squirm, loving the touch, the exquisite scrape across my clit, which is even now quivering to attention, the randy little beast. But it's different this time. I can't settle, can't relax and enjoy because I know what's coming next. Or I think I do. My earlier unexpected reaction to being spanked has already proved to me that pleasure and pain are tangled together somehow, and I daresay I'm about to find out a whole lot more about that. I'm torn between wanting to know, and wanting it to be over.

Standing very close—so close I can feel his chest brushing my nipples—and with the whip trailing down the backs of my legs, he takes my chin in his hand, holding my face still as he kisses me. He is rougher this time, forcing his tongue into my mouth, plunging, invading.

"Are you ready, Miss Byrne?" he asks me softly, releasing my mouth at last.

I don't, can't respond.

He asks again, louder, more forcefully.

I nod, shaking. "Yes, yes—I'm ready."

"It *will* hurt. A lot at first, but don't fight it. And it does get easier as the endorphins kick in. Breathe in between the strokes, and out after each one. I'll give you plenty of time, as much as you need. And I'm going to go easy on you, but if it's still too much you have to tell me. Amber light, remember? I'll help you, you just have to ask. And I'll stop if you want me to." He waits for a moment, lets his words sink in. Then, "So, are we okay to continue?"

I nod. "Yes, I understand. And I'm ready." And this time, I am. I really am.

I hear the swoosh of the whip flying through the air an instant before the pain shoots through me. The blow lands on my right buttock and despite my good intentions I scream. Loudly. Then I gasp, desperately trying to gulp in oxygen as the air has emptied from my lungs, forced from me by the shock. I am whimpering—my bottom feels on fire. I can't help myself. I beg. "Please, please stop. It hurts. Please…"

"Are you safe wording, Eva?" His voice is cold. Like a bucket of icy water, it chills me. I stiffen. I don't want to give in, be sent back to Black Combe. I can do this. I want to do this. Surely I can. I know I can.

"No." I shake my head.

His voice gentles. "Are you sure? Do you want to stop? Did I lay it on too hard?"

Yes!

"No." My response is firm. "I'm fine. It was a shock, that's all. I'm fine."

No more words, but a moment later the whip whistles through the air again, and this time I brace for the blow. It lands, but it's no worse than the first stroke. I cry out again, but I'm trying to manage my breathing, just as Nathan told me to. Maybe it'll help.

"Eva?" The question in his voice is there, clear.

"D-d-don't stop." I am struggling for air, and concentrate on drawing first one deep breath in and slowly expelling it. Then I do it again. I feel strangely grounded, and despite the pain I want to carry on. I *will* carry on. I *will* finish this.

The next two blows fall and my body jerks with each searing pain across my bottom. My whole body is on fire now, the pain close to overwhelming. I clench my jaw, desperate for this to be done, over. He'll stop if I ask him to. Why don't I just ask? Beg?

"H-how many more?" I whisper.

"Ten will be enough. Unless you want more…?" His tone is lighter now, teasing.

"Ten. Yes, ten. I can do ten…" I brace, my body rigid.

"Eva, you're doing really well. Now you know what it feels like, don't fight it. Try to relax your body a little more if you can. I know it's hard, but it *does* get easier. I promise. Let the pain wash through you, blow it away as you breathe out. Do you want me to go more slowly?" His voice is low, and he caresses my cheek as he speaks to me. And miraculously, I'm okay again. More or less—all things are relative. He brushes my lips with his. I feel his breath on my cheek as he asks me if it's all right to continue.

I whisper that it is, and I wait, ready now to let this thing happen to me, to find out where it takes me. I count the blows, my body now conscious of the pain but, incredibly, my level of tolerance increases as I manage to ride each stroke. It hurts, it's definitely not pleasant. But it's not quite horrible either. I'm confused, intrigued and a bit perturbed to find myself becoming aroused again. I hadn't expected that, despite what Nathan told me before we started. I should have, I suppose. He's been right about everything else so far.

The feeling builds as the blows fall, one after another, and I now want this to be finished. Not because of the pain—I'm on top of that, just about, though I'm not quite ready to embrace it yet—but because I desperately want him to fuck me.

"Safe word, Eva? Remember, if you need to stop..."

"I'm all right. Don't stop."

He continues, taking his time, offering me space to gather my wits and prepare myself between each stroke of the whip. I gasp with each blow, but he was right—it is easier now. I'm definitely getting there.

Then it stops. *Was that ten? Really? Are we done?*

After a few moments, I feel his fingers at the back of my head, unfastening the blindfold. He lifts it away and I blink in the light, his beautiful, chiselled face inches from mine. I hadn't realised I was crying, but he wipes my tears with his thumbs, kisses me tenderly.

"You did well, angel. Really well. I really thought you'd had enough after the first couple of strokes, but you're amazing. Who knew a little thing like you could be so…resilient?" *Yeah, who knew?*

Picking up the bottle of water again, he wets my lips, then gently trickles the cool, refreshing liquid into my mouth. I gulp it down gratefully. Reaching above me, he unhooks the metal bar from the ring in the ceiling and I fall like a stone. He catches me, swinging me easily into his arms, and carries me across the room to lay me facedown across the bed. My wrists are still held tightly by the straps, my arms extended in front of me.

I lie still, savouring my relief as my scorching flesh cools to a sharp sting. I wince as he applies some cooling cream, gently stroking it into my buttocks. A thought occurs to me. "Am I bleeding?" I whisper.

"No." His reply is scornful. "What do you think I am? I told you, no blood."

'I think you should be fucking me by now' is my response to that, but I decide to keep it to myself.

Apparently he doesn't need telling. "Playtime, Eva. Open your legs." He lifts my knees onto the bed so I am on all fours with my poor, abused bum in the air, my face resting on the duvet, my hands still stretched in front of me. He nudges my knees apart. I am dimly aware of my vulnerability, my exposure to him as he trails his fingers over my genitals, but well past caring. I want him inside me. Now.

I hear the sucking sound of wet-and-ready-woman as he slides two fingers into me, then three. Incredibly,

I am wet, responsive. It's my response to the spanking all over again, though more intense this time. After the pain—maybe because of it—the pleasure is immense, instant. I clench around his fingers, desperate for more, for harder, faster, deeper. "Yes, oh yes," I moan as he plunges his fingers in and out of my vagina, using my own lubrication to smear over my eager clit.

Then his fingers are gone. I start to protest but his hand on my bottom—which is now only throbbing slightly—tells me to be still. There's a slight coolness as something hard is inserted into my vagina, and something slides across my clit at the same time. Then I am overwhelmed by the glorious tingling sensation, inside me and all around my clitoris, as he switches on the vibrator. Nathan pushes his palm over my entrance, holding the gizmo in place, pressing it to my most sensitive spots where he knows it will have most effect. The stimulation is intense, irresistible. I scream as I shatter within seconds, flying off into the most intense orgasm whilst he watches me, holding me, murmuring encouragement.

Even before the tremors have subsided he slides his cock into me, behind the still-whirring vibrator. "Mmm, the website was right. This *is* great—for you and me. Good choice, Miss Byrne," he whispers in my ear, leaning over me as he starts to thrust. I lose it again, convulsing around him, shaking with the intensity of sensation flooding through me. The pain of a few moments ago was just the prelude, the setting leading up to this absolute joy. This extreme pleasure is only possible because it's delivered in sharp contrast to what went before.

I am starting to see, to understand. My light-bulb moment liberates me. Pain, fear—those are the flipside of ecstasy, each sensation brought into sharper focus, sharper relief by its opposite. 'Gentle fucking' was good, beautiful even, but bland in comparison to the intensity of sensory stimulation I am now experiencing. Every touch, every slide and stroke, every shivering tingle is amplified. Every nerve ending is on alert, standing to attention following the whipping. My entire body now shakes with need, desire, lust.

I can't get enough. I scream for more. And he gives it. His cock is huge, forced into me as well as the vibrator, stretching me, connecting with all of me. Slipping his hands under my knees, Nathan raises me off the bed, holding me there, more fully exposed to his hard thrusts. I come again, shaking, exploding. Shattered. There's more yet—he knows it and forces it from me. I climax once more, this time taking the time to savour the delight rather than be swept away by it. Lowering my legs back to the bed, he leans into me, his chest against my back as his thrusts become more gentle, caressing, calming me as he reaches around me to lightly feather his fingers across my breasts, stroke my nipples, whisper sweet words into my ear.

"Angel, you are so beautiful. So sweet. So tight and hot and brave. You delight me…" I feel the hot rush of semen pumping into me as he climaxes, and I squeeze him to acknowledge it, to accept it, to welcome it.

Afterwards we lie still, both of us facedown, my wrists still bound. Noticing, I flex my arms. "Are you going to undo these now?" I ask, rolling onto my back.

"Not much point, sugar," he replies, lifting himself onto one elbow to lean over and kiss me. "I intend to stretch you out over my sofa in a couple of minutes and see how you respond to that sweet little cane you bought. But let me get my breath back first."

"You must be kidding! I'm done. Just let me sleep."
He's joking, right?

"Sleep if you want, Miss Byrne. For a minute or two.
But I guarantee you'll be wide awake as soon as you
feel that cane across your tight little butt."

Holy fucking shit! Then— *Bring it on...*

I have a sudden rush of blood to my head—that's
the only explanation. "Whenever you're ready, big
boy..." I smile and bring my hands down, dropping
the bar across the back of his neck as I pull myself
against him, kissing him.

* * * *

"Kneel on the sofa, facing the back."

Nathan is gently positioning me for the next leg of
my voyage of self-discovery. The sofa is a dark brown
leather affair, rather boxy in shape. The back is solid,
thick, the cushions flat and firm. It reminds me of the
furniture in a classy dentist's waiting room. "Lean
forward, across the back. Let your arms and head
drop down." I find myself dangling over the back of
the sofa, and am not surprised when Nathan flicks a
catch to release more leather straps from between the
cushions under my knees. Clearly, this is no ordinary
sofa.

Spreading my knees wide apart, he quickly loops the
restraints around them, then produces more straps to
do the same at my ankles. The sofa's back is low, so
the effect is to shove my bottom up into the air, a
perfect target for his cane. I know it's going to hurt.
It's going to hurt like crazy. At first. Just as the whip
did. But I also know I can handle it, accept it, use it.
And the orgasms to follow will be incomparable. I feel
my vagina start to moisten in anticipation. I shift

against the leather, instinctively trying to find a way to rub my clit against it.

Nathan moves around to my head, crouching, lifting my hair to see my face. "Remember your safe words, Eva. This will be more intense. We can stop, or slow down, whenever you want. Understand?"

"Yes, I know. I think I'm ready…"

He raises one eyebrow, glancing up at my naked body, spread out and restrained for his attention. "Yup, I guess you are, Miss Byrne. You do seem very eager, much more enthusiastic than before. Are you perhaps starting to enjoy yourself?"

I feel myself blushing. How can I be remotely embarrassed after all we've done? Seeing my flushed face, Nathan smiles, kisses me, offers me another sip of water. "Embarrassed, Miss Byrne? That's cute. Remember — safe words." With that final parting shot, he clips the bar between my hands to the foot of the sofa, which means I am effectively pinned in place, unable to move at all. He stands, walks around the sofa to stand behind me. I feel his gaze on my quivering bottom even though he is out of my line of sight.

His voice is cool, businesslike. "I won't blindfold you this time, Miss Byrne. You can't see anything from down there, anyway. I do want you to concentrate, though. Are you paying attention, Miss Byrne?"

Foolishly, I don't answer. I should have learnt by now. The hard slap across my butt makes me jerk, and I gasp.

"Miss Byrne. I said 'are you paying attention?'"

"*Yes!*" I shout, smarting. Oddly humiliated that he is spanking me, and keenly aware that I can't move at all — I am totally helpless.

"Good. Shall we begin, then?"

I manage to mumble my response. "Yes."

An instant later, I hear the rush of air as the cane swipes towards me, landing full across both buttocks with force enough to send my whole body into spasm. The air is forced from my lungs and in my current position it's much harder to drag oxygen back in. Torn between screaming and breathing, the asthmatic in me opts to breathe, and the next blow falls. This time I do scream, my fingers opening then clenching tightly around the restraining bar. My knuckles are white, I notice.

"Eva, it's difficult the first time, I know. Remember, don't fight it, let it flow. Tell me if you need to slow down. Or stop. Safe words, remember." Nathan's tone is gentle, reassuring. I take advantage of the brief lull in proceedings to drag in a shaky breath. He notices, comes around to crouch in front of me, lifting my face. "Do you need to stop, Eva? Your inhaler?"

I shake my head, defiant. "No, no, it's not that. I just... You winded me. That's all."

"Are you okay to carry on?"

I nod. *Please, just get it over with. Please.*

He holds the bottle of water to my lips again, dribbling a few drops into my parched mouth, before he stands and walks away. Back around me. Back to his cane.

I concentrate on my breathing. Low, slow breaths—that seemed to help me last time. It works, for a moment. Then the cane lands across my bottom again, the whistle as it flies through the air the instant before contact more menacing, almost, than the white-hot pain when it lands. I jerk, groan, beyond screaming. I thought I could handle it, but this pain is worse, much worse than before. I need to stop this. There's a way... What do I do? What should I be saying?

The swish of air whispers around me and the next blow falls, driving all coherent thought, all sense of self-preservation from me in a white-hot rush of perfect agony.

"Eva, answer me. What are your safe words? Do you need me to stop?"

I can only lie there, suspended in terror, desperate for this to be over. I struggle to respond, to remember what I need to do. Dimly, I am aware of Nathan's voice behind me somewhere, relentless, asking me if I'm okay.

No, no, no! I scream, but there is no sound, my voice paralysed with the rest of me.

Did he say how many strokes? Did I think to ask? How much more of this is there? How much more can I stand? Not much. None…

"Are you okay to continue?"

Like an idiot—a stubborn, foolish idiot—I manage to mumble, "Yes."

The cane whistles through the air again, lands. I lie still in silent, deathly agony. My body is shattering under the wicked, searing pain, starting to shut down. I can't think straight. I know there's something I could—should—do now, but I can't remember how to help myself. The edges of my vision are grey, blurring. I shake my head, trying to get my wits together.

The next blow falls, my only response now a pathetic, beaten whimper. It's too much. The grey darkens, blackens. My world goes mercifully dark, and I feel nothing anymore.

About the Author

Until 2010, Ashe was a director of a regeneration company before deciding there had to be more to life and leaving to pursue a lifetime goal of self-employment.

Ashe has been an avid reader of women's fiction for many years—erotic, historical, contemporary, fantasy, romance— you name it, as long as it's written by women, for women. Now, at last in control of her own time and working from her home in rural West Yorkshire, she has been able to realise her dream of writing erotic romance herself.

She draws on settings and anecdotes from her previous and current experience to lend colour, detail and realism to her plots and characters, but her stories of love, challenge, resilience and compassion are the conjurings of her own imagination. She loves to craft strong, enigmatic men and bright, sassy women to give them a hard time—in every sense of the word.

When she's not writing, Ashe's time is divided between her role as resident taxi driver for her teenage daughter, and caring for a menagerie of dogs, cats, rabbits, tortoises and a hamster.

Ashe Barker loves to hear from readers. You can find her contact information, website details and author profile page at http://www.total-e-bound.com.

Total-E-Bound Publishing

www.total-e-bound.com

Take a look at our exciting range of literagasmic™
erotic romance titles and discover pure quality
at Total-E-Bound.

Lightning Source UK Ltd.
Milton Keynes UK
UKOW03f2348120314

228021UK00001B/40/P